DEAD IN VINEYARD SAND

A Martha's Vineyard Mystery

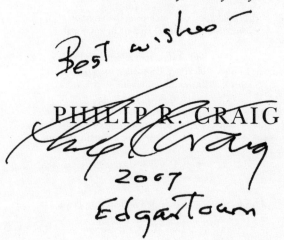

Best wishes —

PHILIP R. CRAIG

Philip R. Craig

2007
Edgartown

SCRIBNER
New York London Toronto Sydney

SCRIBNER
1230 Avenue of the Americas
New York, NY 10020

SCRIBNER and design are trademarks of Macmillan Library Reference USA, Inc., used under license by Simon & Schuster, the publisher of this work.

For information about special discounts for bulk purchases, please contact Simon & Schuster Special Sales: 1-800-456-6798 or business@simonandschuster.com

DESIGNED BY LAUREN SIMONETTI
Text set in Baskerville

Manufactured in the United States of America

1   3   5   7   9   10   8   6   4   2

Library of Congress Cataloging-in-Publication Data

Craig, Philip R. [date]
Dead in Vineyard sand : a Martha's Vineyard mystery / Philip R. Craig.
p. cm.
1. Private investigators—Massachusetts—Martha's Vineyard—Fiction.
2. Martha's Vineyard (Mass.)—Fiction. I. Title.
PS3553.R23D4 2006
813'.54—dc22   2006042245
ISBN-13: 978-0-7432-7044-1
ISBN-10:   0-7432-7044-4

For Bill and Vicki Tapply,
Fly-casters, friends, and fellow scribblers

O what can ail thee, knight-at-arms
Alone and palely loitering?
The sedge has withered from the lake,
And no birds sing.

—JOHN KEATS
"LA BELLE DAME SANS MERCI"

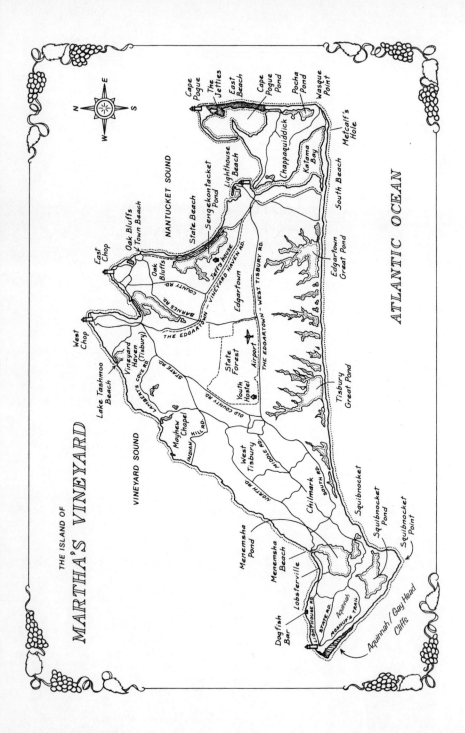

DEAD IN
VINEYARD SAND

— 1 —

We were having lovely June weather. Our children, Joshua and Diana, had only a few more days of school and their mother had already added another pistol-shooting trophy to the growing collection she kept stowed away in our guest room closet. It was still a few weeks before the Glorious Fourth, which would semi-officially announce the start of the summer season on Martha's Vineyard, but already the streets and roads were full of off-island cars. Golfers were crowding the courses, and the beaches were almost full.

At one of these beaches, alas, we'd already had our first drowning: a teenage girl from New Haven who had been partying one night with friends at Great Rock Bight. Almost every year, it seemed, the island's lovely waters lured some unwary swimmer to early doom, reminding us all that our Edenic island was not the perfect paradise many believed it to be. The young girl's death struck us a bit closer to the bone than most because Manny Fonseca, Zee's shooting instructor, knew her father, and the father's hurt had in part been communicated to us through Manny. Moreover, Zee had been on duty at the hospital when the EMTs brought in the girl's body.

But life doesn't stop for death, and more people were arriving on the Vineyard every day. Houses were being opened for the summer, and on the bike paths the galloping moms were running behind their tricycle baby carriages, couples were strolling, joggers were jogging, and even a few bikers were biking.

Bikes staying on the bike paths did not apply to the island's pro bikers, known to me collectively as Captain Spandex and the Tight Pants Bicycle Squadron, who appeared every summer like thorny flowers. Captain Spandex's real name was Henry Highsmith, and he and his cohorts—sinewy, forward-leaning, fast-pedaling folk decked out in skintight pants, bright shirts, and aerodynamic helmets—scorned the bike paths as being too slow and dangerous. They kept to the paved roads, challenging cars for the right of way and taking great umbrage when the irritated occupants of passing automobiles rolled down their windows and screamed, "Bike path!"

I had not screamed that scream although I shared the view of the island plebeians that all bikers, including Captain Spandex and his ilk, should use the bike paths, because our narrow roads, especially the up-island ones, are dangerous even for cars, to say nothing of bikes.

Some, including my rich businessman friend Glen Norton and his golfing cronies, were less restrained when they read letters to the editors of the Vineyard papers written by the Captain Spandex/Henry Highsmith crowd claiming the high moral ground in transportation matters, contemptuously contrasting their silent, nonpolluting bikes with noisy, gas-guzzling cars and especially the four-wheel-drive SUVs that are so popular on the island. Henry Highsmith himself repeatedly extolled the physical, psychological, spiritual, and ecological merits of his daily bike ride from his home in Chilmark to Vineyard Haven, to Oak Bluffs, to Edgartown, to West Tisbury, and back to Chilmark, while condemning drivers of SUVs who made similar trips.

Two such SUVs belonged to my wife Zee and me. We, like many islanders, used our trucks to drive over sand, especially to the far fishing spots on Chappaquiddick and, like other people who live at the ends of long driveways, to plow through the occasionally heavy winter snows. We were quite unapologetic about our SUVs and doubted if Captain Spandex could use his bike to do what we do with four-wheel-drive vehicles.

I was both irked and amused by the cyclist-golfer wars because both sides were so morally pretentious, and snobbery in all forms, including my own when I remember to think about it, offends me.

Glen Norton was annoyed not only by Captain Spandex's campaign against SUVs but also by his other haute-environmentalist views. Henry Highsmith seemed to oppose everything from widening the island's narrow roads, to increasing the number of bike paths, to approving new housing developments, to golf courses in general, including those that were already extant. The last was particularly infuriating to Glen and his pals because to them nothing was more inspiring than undulating fairways, sand traps, and challenging greens.

Thus the letters to the editor from Captain Spandex and his Bicycle Squadron predictably elicited responding epistles from Glen and other even angrier golfers, including one Jasper Jernigan, whose letters were filled with a satirical venom that amused Captain Spandex and his followers not at all, as their answering letters made clear.

"Why do they write those things?" asked Zee, putting down the Friday *Gazette* we'd picked up on the way home. "All they do is annoy each other."

"It's like getting rid of stomach gas," I said. "They feel better afterward."

I knew whereof I spoke, since every couple of years I wrote a letter protesting the annual closing of Norton Point Beach to SUVs by the Fish and Wildlife people in their ongoing vain effort to increase the population of piping plovers. My position was that the closings did next to nothing to help the plovers and were therefore simply another governmental exercise in stupidity; the triumph of dogma over data. My letters accomplished nothing, of course.

"I don't think I'll pursue the gas analogy," said Zee, "although it tempts me to make an odiferous wise-crack."

We had just come home from a Saturday-morning swim and were still in our bathing suits while the kids took turns washing off sand and salt in the outdoor shower. I put my arm around her waist. "Wives aren't supposed to make fun of their husbands. I'll bet Captain Spandex's wife doesn't make fun of him."

"I have trouble believing that Henry Highsmith has a wife," said Zee. "At least I can't imagine anyone marrying a man as uptight and self-righteous as Henry."

"Me neither," I said, although we both knew full well that Captain Spandex was, indeed, married. According to the letters from Henry's defenders, which hotly contrasted his obvious virtues with Glen Norton's and Jasper Jernigan's clear lack of the same, Highsmith was not only an acute moralist and cyclist supreme, but a brilliant Ivy League professor married to an equally brilliant Ivy League professor who, with their two beautiful children, shared his passion for both ethics and the cycling life.

"Maybe we should stop fighting him and join him," said Zee, running her hands up my bare back. "We can pump up the tires on those bikes you got in that yard sale three years ago, and get some exercise." She brought her hands back down and rested them at my waist. "You might lose these love handles you're developing."

"You're imagining things," I said. "I don't have love handles. I'm a perfect physical specimen. Look at this." I released my right arm and flexed it. The bicep was somewhere this side of Mr. Universe's but it looked pretty good, I thought.

"That's your casting and drinking arm," said Zee. "It gets plenty of exercise. I'm talking about the rest of you."

I leered down at her. "Other parts of me get exercise too, my sweet."

She kissed my naked chest. "True, but if the brain is a muscle, Captain Spandex would agree with me that yours could use a workout at least once a day."

I released her and raised my hands to the gods. "Everybody wants me to get exercise. First Glen Norton and now you. I get plenty of exercise."

"How long has it been since we took a long walk?"

"Fishing is exercise. Clamming is exercise."

"How about drinking and napping in the yard?"

"Man does not live by bread alone, and I need my rest."

Joshua came in, drying himself with his big towel.

"The beach was good, Mom. Let's go again this afternoon."

"Why not?" said Zee. "How about going down to Katama so your father can get some quahogs while the rest of us swim?"

"Can we play in the surf?"

"If it's not too rough," I said. "We can go about three, when everyone else is heading home."

"Oh, good! And afterward will you help me with my homework? I'm writing about the color wheel."

"Sure."

Joshua went to his room to change into summer shorts.

"What's a color wheel?" I asked Zee.

"I advise you to beat your son to the computer and learn something about it before you start helping him."

It was a good plan. I said, "Glen Norton wants the pleasure of my company."

"What does he want you to do?" asked Zee.

"He wants me to play golf, of course. Glen can't imagine anything better than playing golf."

She arched a brow. "Well, I guess that might not be a bad idea, if you walk and carry your own clubs. How long is a golf course? Several thousand yards, I seem to remember reading somewhere. If you walk that far, it'd be good for your legs."

"My legs are beautiful and manly just as they are."

Actually, my legs were far from beautiful. They'd taken shrapnel in a long-ago, faraway war, and since then other scars had been added.

Diana came in, wrapped in her towel.

"Ma?"

"What?"

"I'm hungry. Can I have something to eat?"

Diana was almost always hungry, and like her mother she could eat like a bear. However, unlike Zee, who, to the disgust of her women friends, never gained a pound, Diana was growing steadily.

"Change clothes and you can have a sandwich."

"Ma?"

"What?"

"Can we really go to the beach again this afternoon?"

"Have you been talking with your brother?"

"Yes. Can we go?"

"Sure," I said. "The plan has already been made."

Diana smiled the smile that made her look like a miniature Zee. "Excellent!" She went on to her room.

I looked at Zee. "Quahogging is exercise," I said.

She sighed. "Doesn't Glen support that new golf club everybody was so up in arms about? Pin Oaks, the one that's going to cost so much money to join?"

"Another reason for me not to play golf. I could never afford to belong to that club. It's for people like Glen, with a lot more money than I'll ever have."

"They have to build it before Glen can join it, and Henry Highsmith isn't the only person to oppose it. But I know a lot of ordinary people who play golf on the courses we already have. You don't have to be rich to play golf."

I knew those people too. Most of them couldn't afford regular membership in any of the island's clubs, but for a reasonable amount of money they could play at late hours in the summer and more often in the fall, winter, and spring. In the mornings, before they played, you could find them at the doughnut shops, stoking up for the day. We called them the Bold Golfers because they would play in weather that kept normal people indoors.

"What's all this push to get me to play golf?" I asked.

"It's not a push to get you to play golf. It's a push for you to get more exercise." She laughed and skipped away. "Not that kind of exercise! Keep your hands off me. I'm going to go take a shower."

"What a good thought. I'll go with you."

I grabbed my towel and followed her out the door.

Outdoor showers are the best showers in the world. You can't steam them up, they're open to the sky, and the best of them are, like ours, big enough for more than one showerer.

"Allow me to help you out of that bathing suit," I said to Zee. She allowed me.

"Allow me to help you out of yours," she said. I allowed her.

As we stood under the shower, she was a dark Venus rising from the shell, her long, blue-black hair streaming down over her shoulders, her dark eyes looking up at me, her all-over tan making her appear as though she were made of bronze.

"Pardon me, madam," I said, "I don't mean to intrude upon your privacy, but haven't we met before? You remind me of someone, but I can't recall who."

She let her eyes roam over me, toe to pate, then shook her head. "I'm sorry, but I don't think I've ever seen you before. I'm sure I'd remember."

"Allow me to introduce myself," I said, pulling her against me.

When we finally stepped out of the shower and toweled ourselves dry, we felt clean and pure and good, the way you should when you live the simple life on Martha's Vineyard.

— 2 —

One of our favorite beaching spots was at the far south-east corner of Katama Bay, where the Norton Point barrier beach joins the sometimes island of Chap-paquiddick. There, a shallow clam flat reaches north into the bay. It's an excellent and popular place to dig for steamer clams or, if you walk out a ways, to rake for quahogs, two of my favorite pastimes.

Two alternative entertainments are to sit in the sun under your umbrella or wade in the warm, shallow bay water, or to walk across to the south side of the beach and frolic in the ocean surf.

There, when the waves are high, there is danger. The waves can knock you down and break your bones, and undertows can pull you away from shore. Every summer there are ambulance runs from the beach to the hospital, and occasionally some bold surfer ends up paralyzed for life. Worse yet, now and then someone doesn't live to tell the tale.

As you might guess, these conditions make the beach very popular with both native and visiting teens and twenty-somethings, who like the excitement and know that they themselves will never die or suffer harm.

Smaller kids have to be watched very carefully, and are best taken to other beaches when the surf is high. On calmer days, however, younger children such as ours can enjoy playing tag with the waves and floating in tubes at the edge of the sand.

I had my own tube, and floated with Joshua and Diana when the conditions were right for them to leave shore. On noisier days I sometimes played the game called "tubing," which consisted of seeing how high I could ride my tube on a breaking wave without being tumbled onto the sand. It was a sport that required a fine judgment: too far out was boring; too far in was disaster. I liked it for the same reason the teens and twenty-somethings liked high surf, and if asked why a grown-up man would play such a childish game, I referred to Churchill's famous remark that nothing is as exhilarating as being shot at without effect. Old Winnie knew what he was talking about.

We drove there via Katama, which was possible because this year a momentary enlightenment had descended upon the Fish and Wildlife authorities and they had decided to alter their normal policy of plover protection, which consisted of closing the beach upon sighting the first two amorous-looking plovers and keeping it closed for at least ten weeks. Instead, this year the authorities had chosen to close the beach when the first plover chick was hatched and to open it again when the last chick disappeared. The beach was closed for just two days, the time it took for the chicks to be hatched and for predators such as skunks or gulls to find and eat them.

I was filled with hope that such common sense would prevail during summers to come, but wise Zee advised skepticism. "This is a onetime thing," she cautioned. "You're a dreamer if you expect the plover people to be smart more than once in a career."

And I knew she was right.

That afternoon the waves were small, so while Zee and the kids played on the ocean side of the beach, I waded far out into the bay with my wire basket and rake, and collected stuffers and littlenecks. The latter would be appetizers for tonight's supper and the former would be frozen for future chowders or stuffed quahogs.

Raking for quahogs can be almost hypnotically relaxing. You stand in cool water with the warm sun turning you even browner. If you feel too hot, you just bend your knees and dip into the water to cool off. Erect again, you rake steadily until you have your quahogs or you're ready to go ashore without them. It's a task that requires no thought, but allows your mind to float whither it will as your eyes roam the bay, taking in sailboats, distant swimmers on the beach, other shellfishermen, gulls and terns; your ears are full of the sounds of life on the bay: distant voices, the calls of seabirds, the slosh of small waves.

While I raked, I was thinking about Glen Norton and golf and wondering if maybe I should actually take up the grand old game. One thing I liked about it was that, in theory at least, you don't get to blame somebody else if you do badly. Like tennis and chess, and unlike team sports, you can fault no one but yourself for failure; on the other hand, you get all the credit if you do well.

Of course, losers always find excuses for losing: a camera clicked, a flash went off, someone moved or shouted or whispered, an official made a wrong call, someone cheated. Golf, tennis, and chess all produce sour grapes; but still, in theory, you are master of your fate, whatever it is.

I had actually played golf once: a single round in Japan decades earlier when I was seventeen and on my way to be a hero in Vietnam. While we'd waited for transport, golfing grunts, on their way to the same war, had taken me to a misty course early one morning. I'd rented clubs and, knowing nothing about the game but what my friends had told me, had teed up on the first hole and struck a gigantic shot right down the middle of the fairway. It had gone up and over a hill and had disappeared into the mist. It was the first and best shot I ever made, and I remember thinking, There's nothing to this game.

I'd shot 108 and had never played again.

But now Glen Norton was hounding me and even Zee seemed to think it might be good for me. Hmmmm.

When my basket was full, I waded ashore and joined my family. By then most of the other beachgoers were heading home, their SUVs stuffed with sandy people, blankets, umbrellas, balls, beach bags, coolers, and inner tubes.

Later, when I came ashore after a float and a splashing water fight with the children, I told Zee my golfing thoughts.

"And what have you decided?" she asked, handing me a cracker topped with a dollop of smoked bluefish pâté.

"I've decided it's too expensive and that I've got a lot of better things to do in the summertime. Maybe I'll play some in the fall, when more of the local guys play."

I got a Sam Adams out of the cooler and poured some down. Delish! Also illegal, but the beer police were not around.

"Hey, Pa! Hey, Ma! Look!"

Joshua and Diana had followed me ashore and were now standing and pointing out to sea. We looked where they were pointing and saw a dark head moving toward Wasque.

A big seal. It swam then sank from sight, then came up again farther to the east, and swam some more.

Sun, sand, surf, and now a seal. Being here had to be better than being on a golf course.

But we'd no sooner gotten home and showered and changed and rinsed our wet things and hung them out on the solar dryer, than the phone rang. It was Glen Norton, inviting me to play, as his guest, the next afternoon.

"A couple of my pals are coming down from Boston and we need a fourth," he said in his usual cheery voice. "I know you'll like the guys and have a good time. I have an extra set of sticks you can use."

"I haven't swung a golf club since I was seventeen," I said, feeling my mouth water as I watched Zee put ice in two glasses, pour the glasses full of vodka, and add an olive to each. "I don't think your friends will want to stand around while I look for my ball in the woods."

"Oh, don't worry about that. None of us will be playing par golf. Besides, you're in good shape and I know you can hit the ball straight. I've seen you cast."

Zee sipped her drink, batted her eyelashes at me, smiled and licked her lips, and carried the glasses up the stairway to our balcony.

I said, "I'm not sure casting and swinging a golf club use the same muscles."

Glen was full of the confidence that had probably helped make him rich by early middle age. "You'll be doing me a favor and I'll be doing you one. Once you taste the game, you're not going to want to give it up. Trust me!"

"Well . . ."

"Great! See you at Waterwoods at four, then! Make sure you wear a shirt with a collar." He rang off while I was still trying to say, "But . . ."

I looked at the phone in my hand, wondering if Glen's phone technique had also helped him earn his millions. Maybe if you acted like a deal was done, it really was done, often enough, at least, for you to come out ahead most of the time.

I put crackers, cheese, and chutney on a plate and went upstairs to join Zee. The evening sun slanted over our shoulders, illuminating our garden, Sengekontacket Pond, and the barrier beach that carried the Edgartown–Oak Bluffs road. Beyond the beach, white boats moved over the blue waters of Nantucket Sound, and beyond them a hazy stream of clouds hung on the horizon above Cape Cod.

Most of the cars had long since left the parking places beside the road, taking their owners away from the beach and back to their rented rooms and houses. Two ospreys circled above the pond, and a flight of cormorants passed above us, headed west.

"Not a bad spot," I said, glad as always that my father had been smart enough to buy the place when it had just been an old fishing camp, and that I had been smart enough to modernize it into a house fit for my family. I tasted my drink and told Zee about the telephone conversation.

"Well, Vijay," said Zee, "how much are you getting paid to play? You major players do get paid to show up, don't you?"

"If I get paid by the stroke, I should do just fine," I said.

"Isn't Waterwoods the place where Joe Callahan liked to play when he was still president? Pretty posh for a tyro like you."

"I don't think the Waterwoods people care how good you are as long as you can afford the fees. And I don't have to worry about those because Glen is picking up my tab."

"Good for Glen. But if you get lucky, just be sure you

don't get conned into making bets on who wins the next hole."

"I take that as a vote of no confidence in my golfing abilities, untested though they may be."

"As long as you walk and carry your own clubs you'll have my complete support," she said. "I'll even accept being a golf widow if it keeps you in shape."

I sighed. "How soon we forget. Why, just today I thought I'd offered ample evidence of my manly vigor."

She grinned. "Well, parts of you are in good shape. It's the rest of you that needs work."

The next afternoon I drove to Waterwoods. It was the island's prettiest club, featuring tennis courts and a beautiful golf course that wound through low hills and overlooked marshes and a lovely great pond. If you didn't want to play on the courts or fairways, you could have a fine meal in the restaurant and watch the bold golfers whack balls off the first tee. Most of them didn't look much like the pros I sometimes watched on TV on stormy weekends. I was sure I would look just as bad, but knew I could never take the game as seriously.

I met Glen on the practice green beside the clubhouse, where I accepted his spare clubs, shook hands with his friends, and girded my psychological loins.

"Don't worry about your game," said Glen. "As long as we move right along, nobody cares how many strokes you take. You only get five minutes to find a lost ball."

We practiced putts, then we went to the driving range and teed up.

My tee shot went long and straight down the middle, and I thought, Maybe I was right before. Maybe there really isn't anything to this game.

"I thought you said you hadn't played in thirty years," said Glen suspiciously.

I shot 108. No improvement since my last round, but good enough to have Glen ask me to play with him again the next weekend and good enough for me to say yes.

Back at the house, I told Zee about the plan and she frowned and asked, "Did you hear about the fight in the Fireside?"

"No."

"Madge called me from the ER. A couple of bikers and a couple of golfers got into it pretty good. Three of them are in jail and the other one's in the hospital. If you're going to hang around with the golfing crowd, maybe you'd better watch your step. Or maybe you should just give up golf."

I gave her a kiss. "They were young guys and they were drinking, I'll bet. I hang around with an older crowd. We still like our booze, but we're past our punching stage. You don't have to worry about me getting into a brawl."

Famous last words, as they say.

3

"The secret of my game," I explained to Zee the following Monday, "is simplicity. I only use a putter, a seven-iron, and a three-wood. I do all my driving with the wood and all my chipping with the seven-iron."

"And all your putting with the putter, I'll bet."

"You're sharp. That's why I like living with you."

A few minutes later, I had the house to myself, since the kids were in school and Nurse Zee had gone off to her job at the hospital's emergency room.

I used my time to do some weeding and pea picking. Off-islanders are usually surprised to learn that Vineyarders can pick peas in June, but thanks to the Gulf Stream, which usually keeps island winters milder than those on the mainland, we can often plant our peas in March and pick them three months later. Ours were actually snow peas, the kind you eat pods and all, and I planned to use them in a shrimp and snow peas stir-fry for supper.

With the peas and most of the other ingredients safely in hand, all I needed was some shrimp, so I headed down into the village to get them. I could have substituted scallops, pounds of which I had stored in our freezer, but my mind was set on shrimp. By such small things are our fortunes altered.

Many kinds of delicious fish and shellfish are readily available from the Vineyard's great ponds and the surrounding seas, but shrimp are imported, so you have to buy them if you want to eat them. Thus, to the fish market I went, avoiding the newish Stop & Shop grocery store, whose outlandishly high prices offended my sensibilities.

On the Vineyard, of course, all prices are outlandishly high. The explanation, always given with a perfectly straight face, is "freight." The owners of the liquor stores will tell you that's why a bottle of booze costs several dollars more here than on the mainland; a grocery store owner or a gas station owner will make the same claim for the mind boggling cost of his wares. The real reason, as everyone knows, is monopoly capitalism combined with collusion among competitors selling the same stuff.

Since islanders are stuck with this form of robbery, when they go to the mainland they always return with their cars packed full of merchandise; and even on the island, whenever possible, they take small revenges against their most loathed overchargers. Mine, and that of many islanders, was to avoid the Stop & Shop unless I absolutely had to go there. Thus my visit to the fish market rather than to the supermarket for my shrimp. I was in the good mood that the thought of food and drink often creates.

The small parking lot was crowded, but I managed to find a slot, narrowly missing a sleek bicycle chained against a fence. Inside, I found myself confronted by a lean man in a bike helmet, bright yellow and blue shirt, and spandex pants.

"You almost hit my bike!"

I felt my good mood diminish slightly. "Almost, maybe, but not quite."

His eyes were bright. "You people need to be more careful!"

Clerks and customers were turning our way. "Which people are those?" I asked.

"You SUV drivers! Bikers have rights too, you know!"

I peeked over his shoulder at a staring clerk. "A pound of medium shrimp, please." The clerk continued to stare.

The biker moved his head between mine and the clerk. "There really isn't room for you to park there, you know! That's only half a parking space!"

I turned and looked out the window. The space looked big enough to me. I turned back.

"I'm cooking shrimp for supper," I said. "How about you?"

"There ought to be a law against SUVs!" said the biker hotly. "They're a blight on the face of the earth!"

"A lot of people would agree that mine is," I said. "It's getting rustier by the year. Say, you wouldn't be interested in a trade, would you? Your bike for my Land Cruiser?"

Like Queen Victoria, he was not amused. "You're not as funny as you seem to think!" He pointed a finger that almost but not quite touched my chest. "You polluter!"

I thought suddenly that his peculiar, angry attack had less to do with me than with something else that must be on his mind, and that I was just a convenient target. Still, my tongue became momentarily uncontrolled by my reason. "Now, Lance," I said, "don't get all worked up. You'll hurt yourself."

"You'd like that, wouldn't you? You'd like to see me hurt! Well, it won't happen! I can take care of myself! Now get away from me!"

He put his hand against my chest and shoved. Astonished, I went backward two steps. He followed, red of face. "I said, get away from me!" He pushed again, and again I went backward.

I heard my distant voice say, "Take it easy."

But instead, he stepped toward me and his hand reached my chest a third time.

Later, I decided that I should have backed on out the door. Instead, as he touched me, an ancient instinct prevailed. Swifter than I could think, my hands had clamped on his arm and I was twisting it, turning, and locking the arm high across his back in a move I'd learned when I'd been a Boston cop, but hadn't even thought of for years. He cried out and went down on his knees, hard. Customers stumbled away from us.

I stood over him and willed my adrenaline rush away, but held the arm just inches from shoulder dislocation. I put my other hand on the back of his neck.

"Calm down," I said. "Relax."

His head was near the floor. I pushed it lower.

His voice was an angry groan. "You're breaking my arm, you bastard!"

I eased up on his arm a bit. "Take a few deep breaths." I took my hand off his neck.

"Let me go, damn you!"

"Let him go," said a woman angrily. "You're hurting him!" She was the only one of the observers to say a word.

The biker was a muscular guy and I wasn't sure whether he'd come up swinging, but I didn't like holding him there.

"Let's pretend this didn't happen," I said. I released his arm and stepped away.

He rested for a minute, then got to his feet, rubbing his arm and glaring at me, uncowed by his experience. "You can't intimidate me, you Neanderthal!"

Neanderthal? I'd always thought of myself as more the Cro-Magnon type.

"I'm sorry about this," I said. "Let's forget it."

"Oh, no," said the biker. "I won't forget it! You can't get away with this stuff!"

"People like you should be in jail!" said the woman, shaking her purse at me. "You bully!"

I said, "I came in here for a pound of shrimp, not for a wrestling match."

"Give him his order so he'll get out of here," said the biker in an icy voice, letting his burning eyes leave mine for a moment to look at the clerk.

Instead of accepting the suggestion, the clerk put his hand on his telephone. "Do you want me to call the police, Dr. Highsmith?"

"Yes," said the woman. "Call the police!"

"No," said Highsmith, working his shoulder. "Just give him his order and get him out of here."

The clerk frowned but let go of the phone and moved over behind the shrimp display.

The customers and the other clerk watched silently as I paid for my shrimp. As I went out the door, Highsmith shouted, "And don't touch my bike! I'll be watching you!"

"So will I!" said the woman.

I felt my feet pause, but willed them on.

I got into the Land Cruiser, carefully backed out of the parking space, and drove home.

So that was the infamous letter-writing Henry Highsmith. Captain Spandex himself. It was the first time I'd actually met him in the flesh. I wondered who the woman customer was. Whoever she was, she'd either not seen the beginnings of the brief skirmish between Highsmith and me, or she didn't consider it sufficient motive for my retaliation.

If the latter, I thought she was probably right. The store clerk had also seemed to agree. I was getting older; was I getting testier at the same time? The thought did not please me. Years before, after killing a thief who had almost killed me, I'd retired from the Boston PD and come to the Vineyard precisely so I'd not get involved with violence. That plan hadn't quite worked out, though, and now my overreaction to Highsmith had happened too fast for me to stop it. So much for good intentions.

There is a beast within many of us. Usually, but not always, it broods far down in the psyche. Some few psychopaths let it roam at will, but most of us generally build a cage around it and keep it under control. Mine seemed to have gotten a clawed paw through the bars far enough to scratch Henry Highsmith. I didn't like it.

When Zee got home, the first thing she said was, "I hear that you beat up Henry Highsmith at the fish market. I thought you promised not to get into a brawl."

The Martha's Vineyard hospital is also the island's premier gossip center. Every rumor or whisper somehow arrives there almost instantly, and immediately becomes common knowledge.

"That's not quite what happened," I said.

"Hilda MacCleer told me that you knocked Highsmith down for no reason at all, then tried to break his arm."

"I didn't knock him down. I didn't even hit him. And I didn't try to break his arm."

"Hilda got it right from Annie Duarte. Annie was in the fish market and saw the whole thing. She says you tried to wreck his bicycle too."

Interestinger and interestinger. "Maybe Annie can become information minister for Iraq if Saddam Hussein ever gets back in power."

Zee put her arms around my neck and leaned back in my arms. "All right, Jefferson, let's hear your version so I can spread it around the hospital tomorrow."

I told her what had happened.

"Ah," said Zee. "Why don't you fix us a couple of drinks and meet me on the balcony? Where are the kids?"

The kids were in the tree house we'd built out back in the big beech tree, playing something. Doctor, maybe? No, not Doctor!

Before I poured the vodka I went to the porch and spoke to the tree: "What are you playing?"

"Crazy Eights," said both voices almost in harmony.

"Who's winning?"

"I am," said both voices almost in harmony. Laughter fell from the tree house like diamonds.

I fixed the drinks and took them up to the balcony. It was a lovely evening and the beauty should have been enough to occupy my attention. When Zee joined me, however, she said, "You're clouding. What are you thinking about?"

Until she mentioned the cloud, I hadn't been aware of it, but I knew she was right. I told her I'd been speculating about Henry Highsmith.

"And what was the nature of your speculation?"

"I was wondering why he was so upset that he put his hands on me just because I'd gotten close to his bike."

"Maybe he recognized you as the enemy because you drive a rusty old Land Cruiser."

"You think so?"

"Maybe he recognized your face. Maybe he'd read one of your plover letters and knew that you were evil."

"I haven't written a plover letter for a year. No, something was bothering him enough to make him strike out. I just happened to be a convenient target. I wonder what was in his craw."

She sipped her drink. "You're serious."

"Yes." Then I shrugged. "No matter. It's water under the bridge."

* * *

The next day I met the Chief downtown, where he was trying to teach a young summer cop how to keep traffic moving on Main Street.

"Well, well," he said. "I hear you drove your truck over Henry Highsmith's fancy bike, then beat him up when he complained."

"Am I under arrest?"

"Not yet," he said, "but it may not be long." He nodded at a man coming down the sidewalk. "Morning, Dan."

"Morning, Chief," said Dan. "Your young cop is doing pretty well, I'd say. Morning, J.W. Hey, I hear you nearly sent Henry Highsmith to the hospital. What the hell happened, anyway?"

"It's a long story," I said. "You know Annie Duarte?"

"Sure."

"She's my publicist," I said. "I can give you my version, but I expect that hers will be the one to make it into print."

"I'm all ears."

"Well," I said, "it was like this . . ."

When I was finished, the Chief said, "There are always at least two stories, but yours isn't the one most people have heard, so keep your eyes open. We had a couple of fighting bikers in jail over the weekend and there are probably others who'd like to get a piece of you for beating up Highsmith."

"But I didn't beat up Highsmith."

"That doesn't make any difference," said Dan, with a grin.

"You two can tell people my side of the story," I said.

"We can do that," said the Chief, "but a lot of people believe what they want to believe, so be careful until this dies down."

What a world.

4

My old friend John Skye needed no extended explanations when I saw him later that day. We'd known each other too long for that. He was familiar with the Highsmiths because, like them, he was a notable academician when not vacationing on the Vineyard. And even here, ever the scholar, John was researching his next book.

"I can understand Henry being irrational," he said, as we sipped beers behind his old farmhouse. "After all, he's married to a Hatter, and the Hatters have a long tradition of producing oddball family members. They're probably one reason so many people think professorial types are wacky, in fact."

"Is his wife one of the Mad Hatters?"

"Not that I've ever noticed, but I don't live with her. Anyway, I don't think you should dwell on your scuffle. Go home and play with your kids."

"They're still in school."

"Not for long. Go prepare a celebration for the upcoming summer vacation."

"An excellent thought."

I knew just the thing: I would give my children a showing of my priceless video of *Tarzan and the Leopard Woman*. The film had been one of my father's favorites, and by what was surely a miracle, a guy I knew who ran a small movie theater in Maine had somehow gotten the original reels and had made video copies of the movie.

They were, as far as I knew, the only such videos, and I had one of them.

Years before I obtained the video, my father had let me stay up late to watch the film on television. It was a shining memory, and what better gift could I now bestow upon my children than showing the movie to them at the beginning of summer? Great art is timeless, after all.

Still, in spite of John's advice to put my encounter with Highsmith behind me, I kept the Chief's advice in mind, and during that last school week when I was downtown and feeling imaginative I felt eyes on me and heard whispers behind my back: J. W. Jackson, the guy who hates bikers and beats them up: J. W. Jackson, the guy who deserves a beating himself.

Once, shortly after a group of lean, healthy cyclists was going down Main as I was walking in the opposite direction, I thought I heard a voice say, "Hey, guys. That's him! Jackson!" And I had to force my feet to walk on.

But when I wasn't fantasizing I heard and saw nothing truly threatening. I wondered if other people played such odd mind games with themselves and guessed that they did. After a few days, I willed the games away; life was peculiar enough without my making it even more bizarre.

What, for instance, could be stranger than me playing golf again the coming weekend? Two golf games on successive weekends after playing only one previous round in my entire life?

Glen Norton was all enthusiasm.

"You'll never have a boring day, and you'll always have something to talk about. You'll meet new people, and you can play until you've got one foot in the grave. It's the greatest game ever invented!"

I already had very few boring days, and I could always talk about things with Zee. I met as many new people as I needed to meet and sometimes more—Henry Highsmith, for example—and I expected to keep fishing at least as long as Glen Norton was swinging a golf club. But I had let myself be talked into golfing. So much for the life of reason.

"You're not the only mystified mortal," said Zee when I pontificated about life's paradoxes as we prepared supper. "There are some other puzzled people up in the ER."

Emergency room medical personnel know all about the dark side of Vineyard life, as do its social workers, cops, schoolteachers, ministers and priests, and the other underpaid people who tend to the injuries—physical, mental, and spiritual—of the wretched refuse of the island's teeming shores.

"ER people are always dealing with the island's incomprehensible events," I said. The chamber of commerce may pass the Vineyard off as paradise, but the ER people know that it's just as close to chaos.

"In this case," said Zee, "the puzzle may be of interest to you. Abigail Highsmith came into the ER today sporting the effects of a bicycle accident. She said she hit some gravel up near Lamberts Cove Road. Nothing broken, but she lost some skin and banged up a shoulder. Fortunately, she was wearing a helmet."

The police scrape-up crashed bicycle riders all summer long, and a good percentage of the accidents are due to skids caused by sand or gravel. Most of the riders survive with abrasions and bruises, but some also suffer broken bones and there are occasional fatalities, usually from encounters with automobiles.

"I seem to remember that Abigail is Henry's other half," I said, "and I'd expect a Highsmith to wear a helmet. Wherein lies the mystery? Or are you and your medical colleagues perplexed by the idea that a Highsmith can take a tumble just like anybody else?"

"Even Lance Armstrong can take a tumble," said Zee. "No, the mystery is that Abigail claims that she fell all by herself, but the Samaritan who brought her in says she was driven off the road by a beat-up old SUV. The Samaritan stopped to help her but the SUV hightailed it on out of sight."

Odd, but not impossible to explain. Maybe the offending driver never realized what had happened and had innocently driven on. Maybe Abigail Highsmith had whacked her helmeted head hard enough to be confused about what had happened.

"Did anyone report the accident to the police?"

"We did," said Zee, "but I doubt if they can do much more than talk with Abigail and the Samaritan. Abigail's injuries are minor and she says it was her own fault, so I can't see the police doing much."

"So what's the problem?"

Zee frowned. "The problem is that most of us believe the Samaritan and we can't understand why Abigail insists that the accident was her own fault. If it was me, I'd be mad as hell about being run off the road, and I'd want the driver who did it arrested and hung!"

Zee was actually an opponent of capital punishment and of violence in general, so I knew she was exaggerating. But I took her point.

"Are you especially perplexed because Abigail's a Highsmith, and the Highsmiths are death on SUVs?"

Zee nodded. "You'd think she'd be more than glad to nail that driver as an example of the kind of people who drive SUVs. But she didn't. It just doesn't make any sense to me."

I gave her my theory about the banged head, but she

didn't buy it. "There was nothing wrong with her head. She landed on her shoulder."

"Maybe the Samaritan was imagining things."

"I don't think so. She'd been following the SUV for quite a while and saw everything very clearly."

"Maybe she hates SUVs and made up the whole story."

"She drives an SUV herself. What do you think about that?"

"Maybe she's filled with guilt and self-loathing about driving an SUV and was really trying to purify herself. Did you ask her if she's been reading Dostoyevsky?"

"Slice that onion and be serious. Don't you think it's odd that Abigail Highsmith denies being run off the road?"

"If that's what happened. It could be that she hit the sand as the SUV was passing her. She fell and the Samaritan misinterpreted it as the SUV driving her into the ditch."

Zee added my sliced onion to her salad bowl and I began to mix up a dressing. "I suppose that's possible," she said, "but I don't think that's what happened."

"Why not?"

She stopped working and looked up at me. "Because when I listened to Abigail, I knew she was lying, and when I listened to the Samaritan, I knew she was telling the truth. And so did most of the other staff."

Cops and doctors and others who deal with people in trouble expect some of them to lie about their problems, and they get pretty good at smelling falsehoods. Freud probably had a theory about such lies and liars, but if he did I never read it.

When I was a cop, I learned that almost anyone would lie when the truth was to his disadvantage. I also met some who habitually lied to me out of a primeval fear of authority figures. Lies are commonly told to protect loved ones. There was never a murderer who didn't have friends and relatives who would extol his virtues and swear that he was home with them helping a sweet little child with her prayers when in fact he was two miles away cutting someone's throat.

Of course, one of the reasons I understood lies so well is that I lie myself for the same reasons other people do. I ration mine and try to tell them carefully, but I do tell them. My own favorite ploys are to use ambiguity and half-truths as camouflage.

Zee, I knew, was good at recognizing a fib when she heard it.

"You're sure," I said. It wasn't a question.

"Yes."

Hmmmmm. I stirred the olive oil, vinegar, and spices together, then capped and shook the bottle. The dressing sloshed and swirled. I uncapped it and sniffed. Delish.

I thought of the world's accepted liars: golfers, fishermen, politicians. Why not bicyclists? I posed this notion to Zee.

"All I can swear to is that nurses never lie," she lied. "We're the good people."

"When you take off the white uniform and pick up a rod, your fish stories have raised a skeptical eyebrow or two."

She sampled the dressing and found it satisfactory. "I don't have a white uniform, and fish stories are supposed to raise skeptical eyebrows."

True on both counts. Zee wore civvies to work, and fish were expected to grow longer and heavier as they starred in stories.

"Well," I said, "maybe the truth about the Highsmith bicycle wreck will one day be told. Meanwhile, though,

I believe I'll concentrate my energies on my upcoming golf match."

She put the salad in the fridge and checked on the marinating bass fillet that I'd soon be grilling. "Carry your own clubs and walk all eighteen holes. That's all I ask. I'll believe whatever you tell me about your score."

I hadn't told her that when I'd played with Glen the Sunday before, we'd shared a golf cart. "History suggests that it will be 108," I replied.

"That's a good number," said Zee, patting me on the shoulder. "I can't think of any reason why you shouldn't stick to it."

I looked at my watch. Sure enough, somewhere the sun was over the yardarm. "How about a little something up on the balcony while we wait for the kids to come home?"

"You have good ideas, Cornelius. When I'm queen, you may have my bonnet."

I got the drinks and she got the nibblies and we went up.

"Nice," she said, looking out over our favorite view.

"Indeed." Part of me admired the water, the distant boats, and the afternoon sky. At the same time another part of me was thinking it something of a coincidence that Professors Henry and Abigail Highsmith had both experienced violent incidents within a week and that neither had seemed quite rational in his or her reaction.

Maybe the anti-intellectuals of the world were right to maintain that pointy-headed college professors were in fact wackier and dumber than their less erudite critics, and to sneer at them for using hundred-dollar words for ten-cent ideas.

Could be.

After supper, on the kids' last day of school, Zee went off to work the eight-to-four shift, but the rest of us sat down together and celebrated by watching *Tarzan and the Leopard Woman.* It was a smash. The summer was off to a grand start.

5

"I hear you punched out that damned Henry High-smith!" said Jasper Jernigan, giving me a firm hand-shake and a manly grin. "Good for you! I'll punch him myself if he ever crosses me in person! Damned do-gooders like him ruin the world for the rest of us! Damn 'em all, I say!"

I wondered if Henry Highsmith had ever before been thrice damned in a single paragraph.

"Rumors of that encounter have been greatly exag-gerated," I said. "There wasn't any punching out." I extracted my hand from Jernigan's grip.

Jasper was one of our golfing foursome. I'd never met him before, although I'd read his passionate and often angry letters supporting the island's newest golf course proposal: a plan to build Pin Oaks, a champi-onship course in West Tisbury.

Such golf course plans came up regularly on the Vineyard and were recurring subjects of controversy between the pro– and anti–golf course factions. The latter consisted mostly of conservation organizations, citizens with property near the proposed courses, and individuals such as Henry Highsmith, who were self-proclaimed defenders of open space and simpler lifestyles. The defenders of the proposals consisted of golfers, for whom there could never be too many golf courses, and shrewd financial operators, who saw the island as a potential goose laying golden golf balls. The impression I'd gotten from Jasper Jernigan's letters was that he was both financial entrepreneur and passionate golfer.

Now, hearing my dismissal of the reports of exchanged blows between me and Henry Highsmith, Jasper said, "Sure," and gave me a wink and fake punch at my shoulder. Apparently he mistook my arrival at the practice green with Glen Norton as evidence that I shared his own negative views of the anti-golf factions.

I thought briefly of clarifying my position by claiming neutral ground, since I was as sympathetic to both sides of the argument as I was unsympathetic to the pious vitriol of either side's louder voices, but instead I decided to say nothing, hoping to avoid an argument I didn't want to join.

Jasper Jernigan wore green pants and a pink shirt with a popular golfing emblem over its small pocket. The shirt, like mine, had a collar, since Waterwoods held that collarless shirts were, for reasons that eluded me, inappropriate for its players and guests.

Jasper's green cap was adorned with yet another golfing emblem, his bag was full of clubs, and he looked every inch the weekend player. Actually, as I'd learned from Glen Norton when we'd driven together to the course that morning, Jasper played several times a week: mostly in Florida in the winter and on the Vineyard and Nantucket in the summer, but also on famous courses elsewhere, both in America and abroad.

"Jasper is a junkie," Glen had said. "He lives, breathes, and dreams golf. He was probably putting in his mother's womb, and he's been playing ever since. When he got out of college, he got a job working for a guy who designed golf courses, then he got started designing and building and developing courses on his own, and he's gotten rich. He's one of the few really happy people I know. He's spent his whole life doing what he wants to do and getting paid for it."

"His letters to the editor don't sound too happy," I'd said. "They sound like he'd like to wring Henry Highsmith's neck."

Glen had nodded. "I doubt if he'd cry if Henry got hit by a truck."

"That's exactly what happened to Abigail Highsmith," I said. "Does Jasper drive an SUV?"

Glen hadn't heard that story, so I told it to him. When I was through, he grunted and said, "If Jasper has an SUV, it's probably over on Nantucket, where he lives, but I'd better watch my mouth before I get him in trouble."

On the putting green I clearly hadn't improved my stroke. The best I could do on long putts was to try to stop my ball within three feet of the hole and hope that I could sink it from there. Three putts were my norm but fours were more common than twos.

Similarly, on the driving range, my practice shots rarely went as straight or as far as I wanted them to go, so I decided to abandon the temptation to whack the ball hard and to concentrate on trying to hit it more accurately. When we actually began play, however, this decision didn't keep me from hooking and slicing, but only from hooking and slicing as far into the woods as I had previously done.

I was interested to note that Jasper, like Glen, wasn't really that much better at the game than I was. Both of them also used a lot of putts and drove a lot of balls off in odd directions.

Only the fourth member of our group, a taciturn man named Gabe Fuller, seemed to really know what he was doing, even though, for some reason, he didn't score particularly well. Unlike Glen and Jasper, he didn't have a lot to say other than to compliment anyone who made a reasonably good shot and to dismiss his own successes as mostly luck. Fuller was tall and thin and was wearing a Hawaiian shirt decorated with pictures of bright-colored fruits. He wore a narrow-brimmed straw hat, and never got too far from his golf bag or from Jasper.

It was another beautiful Vineyard day, with an arching blue sky and a gentle southwest wind. On both sides of the first fairway the trees moved gracefully in the breeze, and beyond them, through gaps between the tree trunks, I could see the blue water of Nantucket Sound shimmering in the sun.

I thought that my friend John Skye might be right. John, who had done his undergraduate work in Massachusetts, had grown up on a small cattle ranch near Durango, Colorado, and had made annual trips between East and West all through his undergraduate years. It was his thought that the two prettiest places in most towns, particularly those out on the Great Plains, where water is in short supply, are the graveyards and the golf courses, both of which are green oases in otherwise brown, dusty landscapes.

Certainly Waterwoods was lovely, with its yellow sand traps, its green greens, and its green fairways winding between its green trees. Even a nongolfer such as I was could see its beauty. But then I thought again, and knew that some people could look at the course and see only ugliness. The Buddha would probably understand them as people suffering from desire, the wish that things were other than they are. Most passionate activists were such people, I suspected. Their causes might be different, but their discontent was the same.

One thing I liked about both Jasper and Glen was that

they cheerfully accepted their failures, rather than growing sour and sullen when a drive went wide, a chip went over a green, or a putt went ten feet past the hole. Their moods remained upbeat and positive and they were sure that the next hole would be a joy to play. I didn't take my game seriously enough to worry about it and Gabe Fuller played well enough so that he didn't have to worry, so the four of us constituted a pleasant foursome.

By the time we'd played three holes, I had become interested in Gabe's game. He and Jasper shared a golf cart and Glen and I shared another, but I noted that whereas Glen and I often parted company to tend our second and third shots, Gabe's drives tended to stay fairly close to Jasper's, and Gabe helped him find his ball and watched him strike it before going to his own, which was inevitably just a bit farther down the fairway.

Gabe also spent more time than the rest of us looking into the trees or watching the foursomes ahead and behind us. His glances were casual and rarely lingered long, but nevertheless seemed continual.

"The important thing," said Glen, noticing me following Gabe's gaze at the foursome following us, "is to keep moving right along. As long as you don't hold up the guys behind you, you can take as many swings as you need."

"The golf cart helps speed things up," I said. "Zee thinks I'm out here walking six thousand yards, but if I was actually doing that, people would be playing through us every other hole."

"You'd think so," said Glen, "but the truth is that those guys back there are probably just as bad as we are and don't play any faster. It's the twosomes that do most of the playing through."

When I finally holed my putt on the third green I

was already five over par and had used at least a couple more shots than anyone else.

Jasper walked beside me to the next tee. "You ever take lessons, J.W.?"

"No."

"I took you for a golfer when we first met, but Glen tells me you're just beginning and it shows. You look to me like a guy who could play this game, though, but what you need to do is take some lessons. I've been playing for thirty years and I still take them." He grinned. "You wouldn't know it from my game, but it would be a hell of a lot worse without those lessons! Even the pros keep taking lessons. You should do it. No telling how many strokes you'd improve."

"I could use some help, that's for sure."

He grinned some more. "We all can, J.W."

Waterwoods' fourth hole was a beauty. It was a par-three, playing downhill to a small green 160 yards away. On the left of the narrow fairway rose a tree-covered slope and on the right the slope fell away into a vine-filled ravine from which there was no escape. A sand trap guarded the front of the green, and beyond it was a splendid view of the blue sound in the distance. It was not a hard hole to par if you could hit a straight ball but it was a tough one if you couldn't, and a deadly one if you hit into the ravine.

I couldn't depend on my tee shot, of course, but I was smart enough to aim it to the left rather than to the right when I finally got to drive. The result was that I hit it in the fairway just short of the sand trap, which for me was excellent.

Jasper had also aimed to the left, but unlike my shot, his actually went that way, leaving him a tough chip from the trees; Gabe, who'd had the honors for the first time, had landed his ball on the green, and Glen's shot had landed in the sand trap.

Jasper's chip shot made the green, but mine went over it. Then, while the rest of us stood to one side, Glen studied his ball in the sand trap.

"I wish people would use the rake after they hit out of there," he complained. I couldn't blame him for being unhappy because the floor of the trap had a rough, irregular surface, and his ball was down in a dip that would make it hard to strike cleanly. We all made sympathetic noises, glad that we weren't the ones in the trap.

Glen could only shake his head and walk down into the trap. He made a couple of practice swings, then stepped to the ball, wiggled his feet the way some people do when they hit out of the sand, and struck.

Sand sprayed toward the green, but the ball flew toward the three of us standing to the side. I ducked as it went by my ear and down into the ravine.

"Blad dast it!" cried the astonished Glen. "How the hell did that happen?" He flexed his right hand and rubbed his arm. "I damned near broke my wrist!" He glared down at the offending sand and then leaped back. "Jesus!"

I followed his gaze, and immediately understood why his shot had gone astray. Instead of hitting soft sand under his ball, his club had struck something else. There, uncovered by his stroke, was a human hand.

— 6 —

Glen clambered out of the trap faster than I'd ever seen him move. "Jesus!" he exclaimed again. His eyes seemed the size of hard-boiled eggs.

Jasper stepped toward the trap, but Gabe put out an arm and stopped him.

"Everybody stay here," I said. I went down into the trap, knelt, ascertained that the hand was attached to an arm and that there was no pulse in the wrist, and climbed back to the green.

Up the hill at the tee, the foursome behind us was peering down, wondering what was holding us up. I looked at my companions. "Anybody got a cell phone?"

Gabe, who was standing close to Jasper, nodded, pulled a phone from his pocket, and said, "I'll call 911." He, unlike Jasper and Glen, appeared very cool.

"One of us should go up there to the tee and steer people away from this green," I said. "And one of us should get back to the clubhouse and tell the manager what's happened." I found myself directing my words to Gabe. "Can you and Jasper stay here and keep people from corrupting the site more than we already have?" I asked him.

He nodded as he lifted his cell phone to his ear, and I turned to Glen. He didn't look like he was in decision-making mode, so I said, "We'll drive back up to the tee and you'll jump off there and make sure nobody comes down here. I'll go on to the clubhouse and let the manager know what's going on."

Glen blinked and followed me to our golf cart. As we rode back to the tee, he spoke in a small voice: "What shall I say?"

For a man who'd made a lot of money being decisive, he seemed almost childlike. I said, "Say that there's been an accident and that the authorities are on the way, and that no one is to go near the scene. Tell them to go on to the fifth hole and play from there. Say that to everyone who's there and to everyone who shows up. Be firm."

"I don't feel firm," said Glen.

"Act that way whether you feel it or not. Pretend you're Donald Trump."

I left him at the tee and went on to the clubhouse, passing other foursomes on my way. At the manager's office I found a young assistant in spotless golfing clothes. I asked to see her boss. The boss wasn't there. I asked where he was. The assistant wasn't sure and wondered if she could be of any help.

I was impatient. "There's a dead person out at the fourth green. It doesn't look like an accidental death. The police are on their way. You should try to keep people away from the site."

Her eyes widened. "A dead person?"

"Actually," I said, still annoyed, "I only saw a hand and forearm sticking out of the sand trap. The rest of the body may not be under there, but I'll bet that it is."

Waterwoods' assistant managers clearly didn't have to deal with dead people very often. The young woman turned pale, and my impatience disappeared.

"If your boss carries a phone, maybe you can call him," I said. I was pretty sure he did carry a phone because almost everyone does these days. I've even carried one myself, now and then.

"Yes," she said. "Yes." She turned and found a phone on a desk and, after a moment of fumbling, spoke into it. "George, there's an emergency! Come to the office right away!"

I steered her to a chair. "Sit down and relax," I said. I saw a watercooler against a wall and got a drink for her. She sipped it and a bit of color came back into her face.

Five minutes later a golf cart hummed up to the office door and a neatly dressed middle-aged man came inside. His eyes moved from the woman to me. "What's the emergency, Janice?"

Janice nodded toward me. "He'll tell you."

"I'm George Hawkins," he said smoothly. "I manage the course. What's the problem, Mr. . . . ?"

I had the feeling that he was expecting a complaint about the course or some offending employee or player.

I shook the hand he offered, gave him my name, and told him about the discovery at the fourth green, about 911 having been called, and about what my companions were doing to keep the site cleared until the police arrived.

He said, "Damn," thought only a moment or two, then said, "Janice, we're closing down the first nine. Get out there with a couple of the boys and collect the people who are already playing the first three holes. Tell them we're giving their money back and that they can play the back nine for free. We'll use only the back nine until the police give us the okay to play four again. Stay cool, say you don't know what the problem is but that I'm working on it. You all right? Good. Now get going." He gave her a smile. "You'll be fine."

She went out and Hawkins and I waited for the police. In time, they arrived: Oak Bluffs cops and Sergeant Dom Agganis of the state police, accompanied by an ambulance. To their credit, they didn't use sirens.

The police spoke to Hawkins and then Dom came over to me. "You have a talent for showing up when the bodies are found. Ride with me and tell me about your latest discovery." He looked at the manager. "We'll follow you, Mr. Hawkins."

"There's a maintenance road that leads there through the trees," said Hawkins. "We'll take that."

He drove a golf cart, and the police cruisers and ambulance followed him. We paralleled the first three fairways and I could see young men and women guiding golfers back toward the clubhouse. As we drove, I told Dom what I knew.

"I didn't know that you're a golfer," he said.

"My third game," I said.

"When people learn about this, they'll pay you not to play," said Agganis. "Bodies follow you around, and they're bad for business."

"I'm the victim of fate."

"Still, there might be money to be made if you play your cards right. You have to take advantage of chances when they come your way. Are we here?"

We were. We had stopped about twenty-five yards to one side of the fourth green. One branch of the maintenance road seemed to lead to the paved highway that paralleled the first hole of the course. The other wandered on in the general direction of the fifth tee, and I was struck by the road's invisibility from the fairway and green. Good golf course design apparently included hiding roads and other areas necessary for upkeep. Image is everything, as they say.

When we got to the green, Dom assigned a young cop to go up to the fourth tee to relieve Glen and send him back down to the rest of us, then went to talk with Gabe Fuller and Jasper Jernigan, who were standing right where I'd left them.

Jasper seemed to have gotten himself pretty much back to normal, and stoic Gabe remained unruffled. He had one hand on his golf bag and stood close to Jasper. His eyes floated this way and that, peering into the woods, studying the police.

By the time Glen arrived, the photographers had taken stills and videos of the green and sand trap, and yellow tape surrounded the scene. Dom and the Oak Bluffs police were getting Jasper's and Gabe's version of events, and I was studying the trap and the forlorn hand thrusting up from the sand.

Glen and I had both disturbed the trap's surface, but it had been pretty torn up before we'd arrived, presumably because the burier or buriers had ignored the convention of raking a sand trap smooth as you left it. Nongolfers, perhaps, or just in a hurry?

Smart manager George Hawkins, thinking ahead, had loaded shovels and a wheelbarrow in the back of his golf cart, and as I studied the trap, cops began carefully excavating the body. It took a long time because, as any beachgoer knows, sand tends to run back down into the holes you're trying to dig; but they kept at it steadily, taking turns at the shovels and wheelbarrow, and finally uncovered the corpse. It wasn't buried too deep.

It belonged to Henry Highsmith.

He was wearing his usual Captain Spandex uniform: skintight biking pants, an aerodynamic helmet, and a bright yellow biking shirt stained by what was surely blood. His lean face looked almost alive, a sign that he'd not been buried too long. A medic crawled into the hole and briefly examined him, then crawled out again.

"Looks like a single gunshot in the chest," he said, looking at Dom. "But the medical examiner will say for sure."

"Bring him out and go through his clothes," said Dom. "Not that there's much to go through. Do pants like those even have pockets?"

A young cop found a thin wallet and handed it to Dom, who peeked into it. "Driver's license, credit card, medical insurance card, and about forty bucks. Dr. Highsmith traveled light."

"Are we done here?" asked a young cop who was holding a shovel. He sounded hopeful.

"No," said Dom. "Keep digging deeper and wider, in case there's something else down there."

"Like what?" asked the disappointed cop.

"How about a bicycle?" said Dom. "Or maybe another body. We won't know until we look."

"We should get a backhoe," said the cop. "Tell you what: my brother-in law has one. He can dig this whole trap up in no time."

Dom surprised me by nodding. "Good thought. Get him down here. Tell him it's a police emergency."

The cop exchanged his shovel for a cell phone and was as happy as Hawkins was unhappy.

"I know this is a possible crime scene," said the manager, "but I'd hate to have this sand trap wrecked."

"We'll do our best to keep that from happening," said Dom, "but we do have to do some more digging, and then we'll be searching the area in case the killer was careless and left something behind."

Hawkins was a realist, and nodded unenthusiastically. I wandered over to where Gabe and Jasper were standing with Glen.

"How are you doing?" I asked Glen.

"Better. I never saw a corpse before. I was spooked for a minute."

"Anybody would be," I said.

"You weren't," said Glen, "and neither was Gabe."

"I used to be a cop," I said. "But I was shaken up too."

"I felt spooked too," said Gabe. "We all just show it differently."

I didn't believe him for a second. A bit later, as I shifted my position to create the impression that I wanted a better view of the hole in the sand trap, I managed to peek into Gabe's golf bag and believed him even less. For there, tucked among his clubs, was what looked very much like a short-barreled rifle.

7

Our foursome was unanimous in deciding to forgo the rest of our round, and when Dom let us go, with the promise that we'd show up at his office later to make official statements, Glen took me home.

"Where'd you meet Jasper and Gabe?" I asked him.

"Jasper and I have known each other for years, and Gabe came on as his right-hand man quite a while back. Nice fellas, both of them."

"Not everybody thinks so. I know Jasper's the push behind the Pin Oaks proposal, and according to some of the letters I read in the papers, that makes him the enemy of the people."

Glen frowned. "I've read those letters. Those blasted save-the-Vineyard-before-it's-too-late people all want to be the last ones to come here; the world keeps turning but they don't want any changes; they want things to be like they used to be, before there were cars and everybody rode horses or bicycles. Not an honest-to-God golfer in the bunch!" He suggested that such people should all perform an anatomically impossible procedure, and concluded by asserting that the Pin Oaks Golf and Country Club was exactly what the island needed if it was to remain economically viable.

Economic viability was a real issue on the coastal islands, because the tidal wave of money that was washing over them had sent property values skyrocketing so high that working people were finding it difficult to pay taxes on the property they already owned and almost impossible to afford new housing. Already the early morning ferries from the mainland were loaded with workers who commuted every day, and the time seemed not too far away when middle-income people such as cops, nurses, teachers, social workers, and small business owners would be joining them.

I was so ignorant of economics that I had no idea what the future would bring; whether or not we needed another golf course, whether or not the mansionizing of the island was the beginning of its end, or whether or not we should limit the number of automobiles and all become members of the late Captain Spandex's Bicycle Squadron.

I knew I was lucky to own a house. I needed money, but I didn't need much, and I worked a half dozen jobs to get it: house-sitting, fishing and shellfishing, and taking the occasional odd bit of work that some-body always needs done: a little carpentry, a window repair, cleaning a yard and hauling the waste to the dump.

Of course no one is self-sufficient. We all need other people, such as the producers of gasoline and electricity, and I needed the writers of books and the guys who made Sam Adams beer, wine, and the makings for mar-tinis. And I needed Zee most of all.

"What kind of a guy is Jasper when he's not playing golf?" I asked.

Glen shrugged. "Nobody who's made it up the lad-der got there without stepping on some fingers. Jasper's no exception. He can be pretty tough, I guess. Personally, I never came up against him. We see eye to eye on Pin Oaks and we have a good time out on the course. He knows how to have fun, and I like that in a man."

So did I. Glen's good humor was what made him attractive to me. I don't hang around with sour people. Life is too short.

"Gabe seems the quiet type."

"Yeah, he is. I met him in Florida a couple winters ago. He and Jasper seem joined at the hip. Knows how to hit the ball when he has to, that's for sure."

"What's his job with the firm?"

Glen shook his head. "Don't know exactly. We never talk business when we're playing. Gabe's got a cool head on him. Hell, he wasn't flapped this morning when old Jasper and I were freaking out. You like to have a man like that in your company."

"He's steady, all right." I remembered Gabe's wandering eyes and the way he never seemed to get far from Jasper. And I thought about the rifle in the golf bag, and wondered if it was unusual for a business tycoon to need a bodyguard everywhere he went, even when he played golf.

Then I thought of President Joe Callahan's vacations on the island when he'd been in office; everywhere he went, bodyguards and medics had traveled with him; and I thought of how celebrities needed guards to protect them from both fans and killers and how gangsters never walked alone, and I thought that the rich and powerful have probably always needed protection from their enemies.

If fame, wealth, and power created the need, I could safely spend my bodyguard budget on something else. Beer seemed a good alternative.

Zee and the children were getting ready for lunch when Glen dropped me off at my house.

"Well, well," said Zee, giving me a kiss. "That must have been a pretty brisk round." She sniffed my shirt. "You didn't even break a sweat. What a manly chap you are." She gave me a squeeze. "You're allowed at the table without showering first."

As we were all eating smoked bluefish salad sandwiches, Joshua said, "Pa, me and Diana have an idea."

"Diana and I have an idea."

"Diana and I have an idea."

"What is it?"

Diana said, "Now that we're out of school, we have lots of time for the idea."

"Yes, you have lots more time now. What's the idea?"

Joshua said, "We think it would be neat to have a vine bridge like Tarzan and Jane and Boy have in *Tarzan and the Leopard Woman*. We think it could go between the tree house and the balcony."

Zee almost frowned. "The balcony is just for big people. You know the rule."

Diana nodded. "We need a place for the vine bridge to go, and the balcony's the only place we can think of."

While their mother chewed and swallowed her bite of sandwich, Joshua looked at me. "You got a lot of rope out there in the shed, Pa. We could use that for vines. It's strong rope that would do the job."

"I take it that this idea came from the movie," said Zee. She looked from one of us to the other. The children looked at me.

"We watched it the first day of vacation," I said. "You missed it because you were working. There's this great scene where the leopard men are trying to capture Jane and Boy, and there's a lot of fighting up in the tree house and on the vine bridge. We have a tree house and a rope to swing down to the ground, but we don't have a bridge." I looked at the children. "That's the idea, isn't it?"

They nodded. "That's it, Pa. Only we don't have vines, so we think rope would be good."

"Joshua and me could help make it," said Diana. "We don't have to go to school, so we could work all day."

"Joshua and I," said Zee. She looked at me. "I think I'd better see this movie."

Her children thought that was an excellent idea. "You'll like it, Ma! It's good!"

"A classic," I concurred. "No one should grow up without seeing *Tarzan and the Leopard Woman*."

"Then we can all make the bridge!" said happy Diana.

"Now, just hold your horses," said Zee. "We're going to have to talk about it before we decide anything. We've gotten by without a rope bridge so far, and I'm not sure we need one now."

"Aw, Ma . . ."

"I didn't say no, but I haven't said yes, either," said firm Zee. "We'll talk about it later, after I see the movie." She put her great, dark eyes on me and said, "And after your father and I have talked about it."

I took her hand. "It's always a pleasure to have an intimate chat with you, my sweet."

She gave me a huge faux grin, teeth pressed firmly together, and said, "I love being kept up to date on things my husband and children are doing. It makes me feel like I'm important to them."

I held on to her hand and widened my smile. "Mothers are always the center of happy families, and there's nothing better than a happy family!"

Zee surveyed hers and sighed. "Break out your video again, Jefferson. We can have a movie matinee."

The children were delighted. "We can all watch it together!"

The family that watches *Tarzan and the Leopard Woman* together is a healthy family. After I'd washed the dishes and stacked them in the drainer, I got the video from its shelf.

"You'll love it," I said to Zee as I closed the living room curtains and she put the video into the VCR. "Johnny Weissmuller, Brenda Joyce, and Johnny Sheffield. What could be better? And did you know that somebody recommended Cheetah for an Oscar?"

"No, I didn't," said Zee, taking her place on the couch beside me.

The drama unfolded as before, and justice triumphed again, although not without difficulty. If Cheetah hadn't untied Tarzan just in time, heaven only knows what might have happened.

"Well," I said to Zee, when the movie was over. "What do you think? Great, eh?"

"Well," she said, "I have to admit that the tree house looked pretty good. All the dirt on the floor would just fall right down to the ground. Jane wouldn't have to do much sweeping."

"Nice bamboo shower too. Clever of Tarzan to build it."

"I like our outdoor shower just as well."

"Did you like the vine bridge, Ma?"

"I liked it a lot, Joshua, but we're going to have to think about it before we decide whether we're going to build one. Tarzan lives in a jungle, but we don't, so we don't have as many big trees for vine bridges."

"We could fasten it to the balcony."

But that idea was dead in the water. "No," said Zee. "We're not going to fasten it to the balcony. The balcony is for big people. If we have a bridge, it'll have to go somewhere else."

Progress was being made, however.

Family life was the life for me.

That afternoon, while the kids played in the tree house—where else?—Zee and I exchanged thoughts about the bridge and told each other about our mornings. Mine was the more unusual tale.

"How awful," said Zee, when I concluded my narration. "Poor Abigail Highsmith. First she gets run off the road, and now her husband is murdered. Someone must really hate the Highsmiths! But why bury him in a sand trap? That seems weird."

"The cops are on the case."

She nodded, then frowned up at me. "I don't want you getting involved in this, Jeff."

I raised both hands. "Don't worry. I'm not in the game. It has nothing to do with me, and I want nothing to do with it. I have other things to do. Like building a rope bridge, for instance."

"Good. You need to be home with the kids when I'm working."

"No problem."

But a problem was not long in appearing. It came when I went to the state police barracks in Oak Bluffs to give my official statement about finding the body of Henry Highsmith.

When I'd finished my statement, Dom Agganis leaned back in his chair and said, "Am I the only one who thinks it's kind of funny that you and Highsmith duke it out one day and a few days later you happen to find his body?"

There was a short silence in the room.

I felt suddenly careful. "We didn't exactly duke it out, but I thought it was quite a coincidence myself."

His hooded eyes looked into mine. "And it's just another coincidence that a beat-up old truck like your Land Cruiser ran Abigail Highsmith off the road a couple of days ago?"

My caution became a chill touched with anger. "I heard about Abigail, but Zee didn't mention a Land Cruiser. Before I confess, should I point out that there are a lot of old off-road vehicles on this island?

Or should I leave that up to my lawyer at the trial?"

Dom leaned forward and touched his tape recorder. "Maybe you'd better give me your version of what happened between you and Highsmith, and then you can tell me where you were when his wife was run off the road. Or would you rather wait until you get that lawyer you mentioned?"

"You going to Miranda me first?"

"Why not?" He turned on the machine and did that.

Any lawyer will tell you not to talk to cops without legal representation beside you, but I was irked and, like a lot of innocent people, saw no need to keep my mouth shut.

I began to talk.

8

The Boston dailies thought enough of the story to make as much of it as they could, emphasizing the murder-in-paradise theme, the bizarre burial, and the background conflict between the conservationists and the golf course promoters.

The Yale-Brown identities of the Professors Highsmith added spice to the tale, and the photos that showed Henry and their son to be classically handsome and Abigail and their daughter to be beautiful added still more fascination, for no tale is more intriguing to the American public than disaster overtaking the rich, bright, and beautiful.

The now-fatherless teenage children, privileged youth on summer holiday from New Haven's prestigious St. James Manor school, provided yet another focus of the tragedy as they bravely rallied around their sorrowing mother and with fetching innocence fended off the more outrageous intrusions of members of the media. It was easy to both pity and respect them. They were too young to have to face such tragedy, but were bearing up amazingly well.

The reports didn't mention me as a possible suspect in the crime, which suited Zee just fine. She was understandably more than annoyed with me.

"You never, ever talk to a police investigator without your lawyer!"

"I don't have a lawyer."

"You have Brady Coyne!"

"Brady is in Boston. Besides, he isn't my lawyer, he's a fishing buddy, and he doesn't defend people, he tends to estates."

"You have Norman Aylward!"

Norman Aylward had his law office in Vineyard Haven and had been recommended to us by Brady Coyne. Norman could, I supposed, be considered our family lawyer, since he'd done some work for us in the past.

"I don't need a lawyer," I said.

"Your alibi for the time Abigail got run off the road is worthless," said Zee. "The kids were in school, I was at work, and you were home alone."

"I wasn't alone. The cats were here too."

"Don't be flip. You can't prove you were here."

"I don't have to. Somebody has to prove I wasn't."

"That lady who saw the accident might identify that old SUV as yours!"

"But it wasn't."

"She might say it was!"

True. Many an eyewitness has ID'd the wrong person as a perp. On the other hand, cops know that and the honest ones, like Dom Agganis, keep it well in mind. Of course, not all cops are honest and our local DA was ambitious, so Zee's point was well taken. When a DA is ambitious, no one is safe.

I put my hands on Zee's shoulders and looked down into her dark, long-lashed, fretful eyes. "Don't worry," I said. "I'm not involved in any of this, and I don't plan on getting involved. Let's take lunch over to East Beach. We can swim and catch some sun and make a few casts, just in case there are still a few blues around."

She sighed, but put her frown away. "Okay. Get the rods on the rack and collect the beach stuff, and I'll fix some food."

I got the rods down from their hooks on the living room ceiling and went out to the truck while Zee headed for the kitchen. Outside, I peeked around the corner of the house and called the kids from the tree house, where they had lately been spending much time discussing the rope bridge. They came down with alacrity because the beach was just as much fun as the tree house.

The real summer season would start in July, but already, since most schools were out, many June people were wandering the streets of Edgartown, cameras in hand, eyeing the white houses and fences, the flowers and the green lawns, or gazing at the boat-filled harbor.

We drove slowly through the village to Daggett Street, so as not to run over any of the tourists, who used streets like sidewalks and sometimes looked startled to find that cars used them too. On Daggett, where the line forms for the ferry to Chappaquiddick, there were only a few cars and trucks ahead of us.

Most of the latter were filled with men and materials heading to some of the many new mansions being built over there in spite of the protests of longtime Chappy people, who wanted their peninsula to stay as it had been when they had moved there.

But reality is change, so new houses and people were appearing on Chappy as on the rest of the Vineyard, and they would continue to appear; the old days were gone with the wind, like the antebellum South.

More or less pleasantly unchanged were the tiny On Time ferries, so called, some say, because they have no schedules and are therefore always on time. These little vessels look the same as they did when I was a kid, and still sail the same route: crisscrossing back and forth across the channel between Chappy and Edgartown. The people who own the ferries have a gold mine and know it. According to Edgartown lore, when the ownership of the ferry changes hands every decade or so, the sellers can immediately afford to retire.

Could be.

When we got across, we followed the paved road to Dyke Road and took it to the bridge, where I shifted into four-wheel drive and drove on to East Beach, passing the bright-colored kayaks beside the water and exchanging waves with the Trustees of Reservations people as we went by their little office.

"Garish," said Zee. "Brash and tawdry."

We shared a laugh. One of the many complaints the more reactionary Chappy people had, in the seemingly endless winter of their discontent, was that the kayaks rented by the trustees were tastelessly colorful, thus disturbing their peninsula's bucolic natural landscape. These same people maintained that there were too many cars and people on the Chappy beaches, that no bike paths should be built (because they would only encourage more bikers), that no houses bigger than theirs should be constructed, and that, in general, steps should be taken to return Chappy to a mythic, idyllic past when tourists did not visit.

Ah, the golden days of yesteryear.

We took a right on East Beach and drove down to Leland's Point, where we found a half dozen SUVs ahead of us and several fishermen making casts into an apparently empty sea.

We found a place for the big bedspread that served as our beach blanket, and lay down in the sun. The wind was gentle and from the southwest, and the sky above us was pale blue. Thin white clouds blew toward Cape Cod, and I watched some of them grow thinner and smaller until they disappeared completely. It was a cloud-eating sky, a phenomenon I can't explain but have often observed and found entertaining. At a certain spot in the sky, clouds grow small and disappear while on both sides of the spot, other clouds keep right on blowing by.

I pointed out the cloud-eating sky to Joshua, Diana, and Zee, and all of the Jacksons happily watched it devour the clouds that blew into it. It's a gift to be simple, as the Shakers say.

By and by I took a swim, noting as I floated about that the tide was falling and gently carrying me south along the beach toward Wasque Point.

Back on shore, I got my rod off the roof rack and walked back down to the small surf. I had a redheaded Roberts on my leader and I laid it out and reeled it in. No fish. I made six more casts. Still no fish. I looked down the beach at the other fishermen. No one was catching fish. I walked back to the truck and stuck my rod in one of the spikes in front of the grille.

Beneath my feet, the pristine sand was growing hot in the nooning sun, and I thought of the sand trap and wondered how Henry Highsmith's corpse had ended up in it. Someone had gone out of his way to bury him there. Easier by far to leave the body wherever it had fallen.

Who would go to the trouble of burying a body in a sand trap? Was the killer some fanatic advocate of the proposed Pin Oaks Golf and Country Club, boldly showcasing the dangers of opposing the club's development? Or was the killer a clever biker who murdered one of his own and buried him in the sand trap in hopes of proving the evil of golfers? I ran other possibilities through my mind, to little avail. Nothing made sense.

Clearly, the burial had taken place at night, since otherwise the killer, or at least the gravedigger, would almost certainly have been seen by some player or course attendant. That suggested that the killer was sufficiently familiar with Waterwoods to find his way to the fourth green in darkness.

The burial, not the killing, was the real curiosity. People kill other people regularly for all sorts of reasons, but not many corpses end up interred in sand traps.

There was something oddly comic about it all, some hint of cruel, contemptuous humor that twisted the whole affair into a kind of ironic fantasy.

"Come and eat," said Zee, waving me to the beach blanket, where the kids were already gnawing at their food. "I saw you thinking up there," she said. "You weren't thinking about fishing. You're not going to get involved in the Highsmith business, remember? Here." She handed me a Sam Adams and a chicken and cheese and pesto sandwich.

"I'm not involved and I'm not going to get involved," I said. "I mean it."

"Good."

After lunch I was doing some more fruitless fishing when one of the other luckless fishermen glanced at me and said, "Hey, J.W., I hear that guy you floored the other day just turned up dead. Maybe you hit him harder than you thought."

"I didn't hit him at all," I said.

"Sure, J.W. If you say so. You never laid a glove on him. Sure."

He grinned and shook his head and made another cast.

Irksome. I made a half dozen more casts and went back to the beach blanket.

When we got home later that afternoon, the phone was ringing. Dom Agganis was on the other end of the line.

"I just talked with Joanne Homlish," he said in his hard voice.

No bells rang. "Who's Joanne Homlish?"

"Joanne Homlish is the woman who saw Abigail Highsmith forced off the road. She gave me a pretty good description of the SUV that did the dirty work. Fits your Land Cruiser. Are you sure you were at home when it happened?"

— 9 —

"I'm sure," I said. "Ask Oliver Underwood and Velcro. They can vouch for me."

"I don't talk cat," said Dom.

"The lady is wrong," I said.

"What have you got against Abigail Highsmith?"

"I don't know her. I've never seen her."

"Why don't you drive up here and see me? Now would be a good time."

I wondered what burr was under Dom's saddle. Maybe he'd tell me. "I'm on my way," I said.

"What was that all about?" asked Zee, frowning.

I told her, then said, "Don't worry. Dom is a smart guy. He knows I wasn't up-island when Abigail High-smith crashed."

"Dom is a cop," said Zee, frowning still more. "You shouldn't be talking to him without a lawyer."

"I don't need a lawyer to find out what's bothering Dom," I said. "I'll be back soon."

"If you won't call Norman Aylward, I will," said Zee, and she was walking toward the phone when I went out the door.

The state police barracks is on Temahigan Avenue in Oak Bluffs, not far from the Martha's Vineyard hospital where Zee works. The building was for many years painted a rather garish blue but is now shingled in weathered cedar and looks much more Vineyardish. I parked in the lot in back and went into Dom's office. He and his underling, Officer Olive Otero, were both there.

Olive and I, for some reason, had never hit it off. We were like oil and water, fire and ice, Rome and Carthage. Dom and I, on the other hand, had gone fishing together now and then.

Now, Dom waved me to a chair in front of his desk while Olive eyed me without affection.

"What's gotten your feathers ruffled?" I asked, sitting down.

"This," said Dom. He handed me a stack of photographs of old and young jeeplike vehicles. "Joanne Homlish went through these and picked out your truck without even hesitating. She knows what she saw."

I went through the pile and there, sure enough, was a photo of a Toyota Land Cruiser. The truck in the photo was new when the picture had been taken years before and it was painted yellow, whereas mine was ancient, rusty, and faded blue; but it was a picture of my vehicle model, all right. I looked in the small print and confirmed that the truck in the picture was a 1961 model. Bingo again.

"Where do you come up with this stuff?" I asked. "I thought you only kept mug shots and fingerprints."

"The arm of the law is long," said Dom. He leaned forward on his elbows. "Well, what do you say now? How many 1961 Land Cruisers do you think there are on this island, anyway? Do you still say you were at home with the kitties that afternoon?"

I glanced at Olive, saw a grim smile on her face, and looked back at Dom. "There are a lot of old off-road vehicles on the island and I was home with the kitties. Does Joanne Homlish wear glasses? Does she drive with them or just read with them?"

"She gave me the name of her optometrist and I

called him. He says all she needs to read are those drugstore specs and that her distance vision is fine."

"Was she sober?"

"As a judge." Then he seemed to remember some of the judges with whom he'd had dealings, and added, "I'm speaking figuratively, of course."

"Was she high on something?"

"No."

"Had she forgotten her medication?"

"No."

"In that case, she's either lying or imagining things or there's another truck that looks like mine here on the island. I imagine there are several."

He stared at me. "You ever hear of Occam's razor?"

I couldn't resist gesturing toward Olive. "Everybody but Olive, here, has heard of Occam's razor. You're pushing the notion that the simplest explanation that's consistent with the facts is probably the truth."

He nodded. "It usually works out that way."

I smiled at Olive and saw that she was seething, then looked back at Dom. "In this case one fact doesn't fit: I was home with the cats and my truck was with me." I had a thought. "Say, Joanne Homlish isn't one of those plover people, is she? The ones who think I'm Satan himself when I complain about the Norton Point Beach being closed every summer so the plover chicks can fledge?"

"Easy, Olive," said Dom. "No, J.W., she's not one of those people. In fact, when your name came up, she said she'd never heard of you."

So much for revenge as a motive for lying about me and my truck. Of course, Joanne might have had her own reasons for doing it, but I remembered Zee saying that she believed the woman who'd seen the accident.

Olive could restrain herself no longer. "Why don't

you save us a lot of time and effort and come clean, Jackson? We know it was you!"

I didn't look at her. "You don't even know how to spell your name, Olive. Now be quiet before Dom has to send you to your room."

"You . . . !"

"Stop it!" said Dom. "Both of you!"

"Sure," I said, and smiled again at Olive, who was pushing her lips together so hard they looked like they hurt, while her eyes blazed at me.

"Just so you'll know where you stand," said Dom, "I showed her a picture of you, but she didn't recognize you."

"Because I wasn't there."

"Because all she saw was the back of the driver's head. The reason I'm not pushing this harder is because Abigail Highsmith insisted that nobody drove her off the road, that she just had an accident."

We stared at each other. Then I said, "But you don't believe her."

He shrugged.

I said, "You don't believe her, but you do believe Joanne Homlish."

"And we don't believe you, either," snapped Olive, unable to hold her tongue another moment.

"Which brings me to my earlier question," said Dom, waving a silencing forefinger at Olive. "What have you got against Abigail Highsmith? I know that you and her husband had a scuffle, but what's that got to do with Abigail?"

"Yeah," said Olive, ignoring the forefinger. "Were you so sore about her husband that you decided to take it out on her? That sounds like something you might do!"

"Dom," I said. "You should keep your attack dog

here caged at least until you feed her. Loose and hungry like this, she's liable to bite herself to death."

"I said to stop it!" said Dom, this time in his I-don't-want-to-say-this-again voice.

"Sure," I said. "No problem. Back to your question, I don't have anything against Abigail. Like I said, I've never even met her. For that matter, I only saw her husband that one time in the fish market, and I wouldn't have known who he was if somebody hadn't identified him."

"You saw him again in the sand trap."

True. "You're right. I was there when you dug him up. That's twice, I guess."

"Tell me again about the scuffle in the fish market," said Dom.

Police often have people tell them about events several times, in case details change. And they often do, because the people remember things they'd forgotten or forget things they'd remembered before. Or, if they're lying, they lie differently, adding or subtracting or changing what they'd said before. Out of all this, the police hope to find out what really happened.

I told him what happened. When I was done, he said, "That's not how Annie Duarte saw it. She says you started it and would probably have killed Highsmith if you hadn't had witnesses."

I was already annoyed with Annie Duarte. I said, "Annie Duarte and Joanne Homlish aren't sisters, are they? Neither one of them seems to know what she's looking at."

Dom smiled coldly. "They may make good witnesses in court."

Court had not been mentioned before. "There were several people in the fish market," I said. "Annie Duarte isn't the only one who saw what happened. Check out some of the other witnesses before you decide what really went on."

"You don't need to tell us how to do our job!" snapped Olive.

"This is the third time I've told you two to cut that crap," said Dom in a mild voice that deceived no one. "I'm not going to say it again." He looked at Olive and she seemed to shrink inside her uniform. Then he looked back at me.

"Officer Otero is correct," he said. "I don't know yet what's going on here, but we have a probable murder and a possible assault that may be linked, and you've been tied to both victims. If I were you, I'd give thought to getting myself a lawyer. Meanwhile, stay out of our way and let us handle this."

"Sure," I said, hearing anger in my voice. "You already think I may be involved in both of these felonies, but you want me to trust you to do your jobs. I'd trust you a lot more if you hadn't already made up your minds!"

Dom's voice was intended to be soothing. "Nobody's mind has been made up, J.W."

I stared at him and he stared back. I tried to push my anger and fear away, but only partially succeeded.

"Are we through here?" I asked.

Dom nodded. "For the time being, but don't take any long trips. I may want to talk with you again."

"I live in paradise," I said. "Why would I want to leave?" I got up and went to the door and stopped. "I had nothing to do with Highsmith's death or his wife's accident," I said.

"So you say."

I went out, feeling Dom's cold eyes and Olive's hot ones on my back.

As I drove home, I fought against both my fear and

my anger. I felt trapped. I didn't like it, and worked to control my emotions before I got back to the house.

There, Zee was preparing supper. She stopped and came to meet me. "What happened, Jeff?"

I put my arms around her. "Nothing, really. Dom just wanted to go over some old stuff again. You know how cops are. They like to be sure of things."

"I phoned Norman Aylward. We have an appointment with him tomorrow afternoon."

"Fine," I said. "I'm sure we won't need his help, but it won't hurt to let him know what's going on."

"Good. I'll feel a lot better if Norman's working for us." Zee kissed me and went back to the stove.

I went into the bedroom and dug a phone book out of the drawer in the bedside table. There, right where it should be, was a telephone number and a West Tisbury address for Marty and Joanne Homlish. I then looked for Annie Duarte, but although there were a lot of Duartes on Martha's Vineyard, there was no Annie listed. No matter; I could find her when I needed to. While I was at it, I looked for a Henry Highsmith, and found only one. He had lived off Middle Road in Chilmark. Two hits in three tries. If the noose I felt around my neck didn't start loosening soon, I'd know where to begin unknotting it.

10

"Pa."

"What, Joshua?"

Zee had already left for work, but the kids and I were still eating blueberry pancakes and maple syrup for breakfast.

"Have you decided about the rope bridge?"

The rope bridge. My mind might be filled with Highsmith thoughts, but my children were thinking about Tarzan's tree house. Which subject was most important? Actually, I'd spent some time planning a possible rope bridge. My musings about Highsmith's body had shunted those plans aside, but now Joshua and Diana had brought them back. What we adults consider real life often commands our attention, but sometimes children's fancy must reign.

In fact, my children's lives were as real to them as mine was to me, and their happiness was at least as important as mine. It was clear that my Highsmith worries and plans were intruding upon my parental pleasures and duties, so I pushed them away. They didn't go far or go easily, but they did withdraw a bit.

"Your mother and I have talked about it," I said. "After breakfast we can take a look outside and I'll tell you what I have in mind."

Diana licked syrup from her lips. "Good, Pa. If we have a rope bridge we can have fun all summer!"

"You have fun all summer anyway."

"Yes, but this will be even funner!" She grinned her miniature Zee grin and stuffed another forkful of pancake into her sticky mouth.

So, after I'd washed and stacked the breakfast dishes, we went out into the warm summer morning.

The tree house we'd built up in our big beech was very popular with Joshua and Diana and most of their friends, and so far nobody had broken any bones falling out of it. There was a ladder leading up to it through a trapdoor in the floor of its porch, so if you were attacked you could shut the door and keep the bad guys out, and there was a rope you could use to swing down to the ground. The porch was in front of the main room and there were two smaller rooms on adjoining branches so the kids could have places of their own. It's important to have a room of one's own, as well as a common room for group activity.

Zee and I had occasionally accepted an invitation to spend a family night in the tree house, but even the main room was a bit too small for us to stretch out, and though we'd used air mattresses along with our sleeping bags, we didn't sleep well.

"First," I said now, "we're not going to have a bridge that leads to the balcony. The balcony is for big people, and if we have that kind of bridge, you guys will use it even if you don't think you should because what good's a bridge unless you can use it?"

"We thought of another place it could go, Pa."

"Where, Joshua?"

"There," said Diana, pointing. "Over to that tree."

"Yes," said her brother, nodding. "Over to that tree right there."

What smart children. That was exactly my own plan. Like father, like child!

"Good," I said, admiring their choice of oak tree. "I

think that would be perfect. We can build a platform in that tree so you'll have a place to stand when you cross the bridge, and then we can make a trapdoor in the platform and a ladder leading down to another little rope bridge that leads down to the ground."

"Excellent!" said Joshua.

"It will be like a back door," said his sister. "Just like we have in our real house."

"And we can lock the trapdoor if somebody tries to get in."

"Yes, you two will have to check and make sure the trapdoor is locked if you don't want unexpected guests."

"Like leopard men, Pa?"

"I think the leopard men were just make-believe people in the movie, Diana, but you can pretend there are real ones."

We went out to the stockade-fence corral behind the house, where I keep materials that are too big to store inside. These include five-gallon plastic buckets, potentially useful scraps of lumber and plywood, ropes, rusty outdoor tools, and other stuff still too good to take to the dump.

Such collections are sure signs that their owners, like me, grew up without too much money, for poor people can never be sure when they might need something. In every poverty-stricken section of America from Maine to California, including some places on Martha's Vineyard, you can find yards full of such materials—broken box springs, rotting piles of unidentifiable rubbish, rusted cars up on blocks with their hoods open from the last time something was pirated from their engines, snowmobiles, old automobile axles and wheels, toys, and rotting pieces of wood.

I tried to make sure I didn't keep any really useless

stuff, and I hid my materials behind the fence, but as had my father before me, I had a collection that no person of means would even consider keeping

Now my children and I entered the corral and found just what we needed to start the bridge: a fifty-foot length of green three-inch hawser that I'd salvaged off the beach following a three-day gale years before. It was flotsam or jetsam off some oceangoing vessel, and I had lugged it home because you never know when you might need fifty feet of three-inch hawser. And now the time had come. It was perfect.

"I figure that oak tree is about twenty-five feet from the tree house," I said, looking up into the trees. "After we build the platform, we can string this big hawser between there and the tree house, and we'll have enough left over to make the other little bridge down to the ground. It's so strong that we'll never have to worry about it breaking."

"But we'll fall off, Pa," said practical Diana.

"No, you won't," I said, and pulled the lid off a fifty-gallon plastic garbage barrel. "Look here." Inside, dry and as good as when I'd put them in there, were coils of rope that I'd picked up here and there in my travels. When you're a sailor and you live on an island, you can never have too much rope. "After we get the hawser strung up, we'll string some of these lighter ropes on both sides of it for handholds, and then we'll tie short pieces of rope between them and the big rope to make sort of a net, and then, look here—" I opened another garbage barrel and revealed the mass of old fishing nets I'd salvaged and carefully stored away just in case—"we'll string this netting over the hawser and tie it to the handholds so you can't fall through. And then I'll get some boards and fasten them to the hawser and make a walkway inside the netting."

But Diana was looking up into the trees with narrowed eyes. "I don't get it, Pa."

"You will when you see the drawings," I said. "Every job starts with drawings. Remember the ones we made for the tree house? I'll make some for the bridge, and then you'll see what I mean." I studied my collection of still-usable scraps of wood: pieces of plywood, lengths of two-by-fours and two-by-sixes, and the rest. "I think I'm going to have to buy some more wood for the platform. I'll know more when I finish drawing the plans."

"We'll help you, Pa!"

"Good." We went into the house.

By noon I had a sketch of the rope bridge that clarified Diana's thoughts on the subject, and I had a drawing of the platform in the oak tree that informed me I was definitely going to need some more wood for construction and some more bolts and lag bolts and big nails. Both the kids and I considered the morning well spent.

I fixed us lunch and was conscious again of how much more I enjoyed the innocence of my children than the calculated business of adults, how much more important and immediate their rope bridge seemed than the violent events that threatened to entangle me in the death of Henry Highsmith and in his wife's accident.

I felt sorry for the Highsmith children, who in a single week had lost one parent and had nearly lost the other. They were older than Joshua and Diana, but were still only in their teens, and they must be suffering greatly from the calamities that had befallen them and had so transformed their lives. Being beautiful and rich had not kept sorrow and chaos from their door. I didn't know if the innocent suffer more than the guilty—Dostoyevsky would probably have doubted it—but I knew that I pitied the innocent more, and didn't ever want my own children to hurt more than they had to.

After lunch the kids and I got into the Land Cruiser and drove to Cottle's lumberyard in Edgartown, where I got the supplies we needed. Home again, we carried our boards and nails and bolts out to the oak tree and parked them there. Then the kids watched while I got tools from the shed and my long ladder from the corral, and climbed into the tree to make my first measurements. By the middle of the afternoon, with the children handing me the tape measure, my handsaw, my hammer and nails, and other gear, I had two-by-six weatherproofed boards firmly lag-bolted around the trunk of the tree.

It was a good beginning, and we were all tired, so we put away the tools and went into the house for lemonade. There we rested in that comfortable camaraderie shared at the end of a day by hardworking people in the fields or the factory. I have often thought that I'm a born sloth, but I must admit that my happiness is often greatest when I've been working hard, "work" being something that needs or merits doing whether we like it or not.

Building a rope bridge was something I liked.

Being involved in the Highsmith tragedies was something I didn't like, but it seemed to me that I had only two real choices: I could trust Norman Aylward to tend to my security and the police to discover the real perpetrators in the Highsmith affair—presuming that Henry's death and Abigail's accident were closely related parts of a single scenario; or I could take arms against a sea of troubles.

But was I Hamlet or just an attendant lord, full of high sentence but a bit obtuse?

"Pa."

"What, Diana?"

"Is the rope bridge going to be done tomorrow?"

"No. First I have to build the platform in the oak tree. This is a big job and it'll take some time."

"How long, Pa?"

How long, indeed? A long time, maybe, if Dom Agganis decided to arrest me for assault or even murder. I didn't think that would happen, but we live in a world that's not always rational.

I looked at my watch. Time to meet Zee at Norman Aylward's office in Vineyard Haven.

"It'll take several days," I said. "I can't spend all of my time working on the platform and the bridge. I have other jobs to do too."

"I hope it's soon, Pa."

"I hope so too. Meanwhile, you and Joshua and your friends can play in the tree house and you can tell your friends about the bridge. Come on, now, I have to go see our lawyer." We went out to the Land Cruiser.

"Can we tell our friends about the leopard men too?"

"Sure."

"Hey," said Joshua. "I just thought of a good idea! We can put the TV in the tree house and watch *Tarzan and the Leopard Woman* there! That would be even more fun than watching it here!"

In the rearview mirror I saw Diana give her brother an admiring glance for thinking of something that she hadn't thought of first. "That would be really good, Pa! Can we do it?" She looked at me with melting eyes, but I refused to melt.

"I don't think so. We only have that one little television set, and that one old VCR, and they're going to stay right where they are."

"Aw, Pa . . ."

Had I made a mistake introducing them to the

movie? As I drove I considered this dire thought. Then I decided, no, you're never too young for Tarzan. Especially if you have a big beech tree in your yard and a house up in its branches.

"If you want," I said, "we'll watch the movie again and you can invite your friends over to see it. What do you think of that idea?"

They brightened. "That'll be good! Then we won't have to explain things to anybody!"

My thought exactly. If everybody's seen the same movie, everybody knows what's going on when you start playing the game.

Thoughts of the Highsmiths were back in my mind when Zee met me and the kids outside Norman Aylward's office and all of us went in. Norman's secretary accepted custody of the children while Zee and I entered Norman's inner office.

"Jeff is involved in the Highsmith case," said Zee, giving me a sharp look and getting right to the point. "I think he needs to talk with you."

Norman wore his lawyer's face. "I've heard something about J.W. and the Highsmiths," he said. "Suppose you tell me everything, J.W."

So I did that, starting from the incident in the fish market and ending with my latest meeting with Dom Agganis, with Zee filling in details I didn't think important. When we were done, Norman said, "Well, I don't think you're in any real trouble yet, J.W. I think the police are just feeling around. They don't have any evidence that will stand up in court and they know it. Just go home and tend to your usual affairs, and with luck the police will find the real killer fairly soon and they'll forget all about you. Meanwhile, if they want to talk with you again, give me a call and I'll deal with them."

"There," said Zee, as we left. "I feel better. Don't you?"

Actually, I did.

Back home, while Zee was changing into shorts, I got the vodka out of the freezer and poured us drinks, put crackers and pâté beside the glasses on a tray, and took everything up to the balcony. As I went up, I heard the phone ringing behind me.

I planned to tell Zee about the progress we'd made on the rope bridge, but when she joined me, she spoke first.

"They brought Abigail Highsmith to the ER while we were at Norman's office. Somebody shot her when she was leaving the funeral home this afternoon after she'd made arrangements to bury her husband. They've flown her to Boston."

11

Olive Otero didn't think much of my alibi when I offered it to Dom the next morning.

"Joshua and Diana are right out there in my truck, waiting for me to finish this interview," I said. "They'll tell you where I was all day. Or you can check out Cottle's lumberyard. I bought supplies there yesterday and I can show you some of them up in that oak tree where I was working during the afternoon."

Dom looked at me. "Did you come here just to tell me you didn't shoot Abigail Highsmith?'

"And to point out that if I didn't shoot her, I probably also didn't try to run her off the road and probably also didn't bury Henry in that sand trap. How's Abigail doing?"

He shrugged. "She's still alive."

"How'd it happen?"

"None of your business," said Olive.

"She and the children were making funeral arrangements for Henry," said Dom. "The boy and girl had gone ahead to the car when Abigail came out the front door. Shooter seems to have been standing in the bushes across the drive. Used a twenty-two and took just one shot. The funeral director heard a pop and glanced out a window as she went down. He ran out without thinking and must have spooked the gunman away. Probably saved her life. When we talked with him he was still shaking like a leaf. It had never occurred to him that there was a guy with a gun out there, and he got scared later."

I didn't blame him. "Rifle or pistol?"

"Pistol, probably. We found one casing. A bigger-caliber gun would probably have killed her."

"Witnesses?"

"The kids were in the car and didn't see anything and neither did anybody we've talked to so far, but maybe we'll find one of those little old ladies who spends her time looking out her window to keep track of what the neighbors are up to."

"How are the kids taking it?"

"They seem traumatized. No emotions at all. Like they're in a dream. First their father and now their mother. The only adults left to look after them were the housekeeper and her husband, but now Abigail's sister and her husband have flown in from Providence. The husband is with the kids here on the island and the sister is with Abigail in Boston."

People get killed all the time and the motive is usually commonplace, but it was unusual for a husband and wife to be targeted by a killer at different times.

"Was the same gun used in both shootings?" I asked.

"We don't know yet, but I wouldn't be surprised."

If Dom was right, the killer had a lot of confidence. He killed once, then kept the same gun and used it again. It would have been safer to chuck the first gun off a bridge so that no one could find him with it or be able to trace it, and to use another one the second time and then ditch that one too. Another possibility was that our killer was dumb. Criminals, even the smart ones, famously do stupid things.

"Somebody must be pretty mad at the Highsmiths," I said. "You usually don't get dangerous enemies like that unless you've done something to anger or threaten them. Henry or Abigail could each have gotten into somebody's sights, but it's unlikely that both of them would have."

Dom leaned back in his chair. "Maybe passions run high in the groves of academe. Henry had a temper, as you should know. Maybe Abigail was just as bad. Maybe they really pissed off a dean or a student or something. People in Providence and New Haven are checking that out."

I thought back to the scene in the fish market. "It was my impression that when Henry got pushy with me, he was already mad about something and was just taking it out on me."

"He got mad because you started a fight with him," said Olive.

I ignored her. "And didn't Abigail insist that nobody had forced her off the road even though Joanne Homlish vowed that someone did? Doesn't that make you think something strange was going on that each of the Highsmiths knew about but didn't want to discuss?"

"Like what?" asked Dom, lacing his thick fingers behind his thick neck.

I didn't know and said so.

"No surprise there," said Olive. "Is there anything you do know?"

"Not much as far as this business goes," I said. "Dom, do you know if Henry Highsmith played golf?"

He arched a heavy brow. "No, but I know that he did a lot of railing against this Pin Oaks proposal and made himself a lot of enemies doing it."

I said, "Do you think there's something funny about Henry Highsmith being buried in a sand trap and his wife being shot coming out of a funeral parlor?"

"There's nothing funny about murder," snapped Olive.

I nodded. "You and I may not think so, but I believe your killer thinks it's a good joke to bury a golf hater on a golf course and to kill a woman at a funeral home. It's twisted humor, but it's humor."

She wasn't biting. "How about the bicycle accident? What's funny about that?"

"Bike enthusiast killed in biking accident. Your killer likes irony. It amuses him."

"It's childish!"

"A lot of killers are childish, Olive."

"I've read Kohlberg. I know his theory." Her voice was sharp but her face had become thoughtful.

I was surprised by her reading tastes but probably shouldn't have been. People are almost always different than you think they are, and Olive was apparently no exception.

"I know you've talked with some people already," I said. "Did you happen to find out why Henry Highsmith was in the Edgartown fish market when he tangled with me?"

Dom tilted his head. "No, I didn't, but my guess would be that he went there to buy fish."

"Yeah," said Olive.

"Yeah, probably," I said. "But why there?"

Dom's head stayed tilted. "What are you getting at?"

I said, "I mean that the only Henry Highsmith I found in the phone book lives up in Chilmark. The nearest fish market is right there in Menemsha, but Henry rode all the way to Edgartown on his bike to buy fish. Why?"

Dom and Olive looked at each other.

"In a couple of his letters Highsmith made a big deal out of his daily ride from home through the three down-island towns and back again," said Olive. "He probably wanted fish for supper, so he decided to buy it in Edgartown."

"Maybe he always buys his fish at that market. We'll see if we can find out," said Dom. "You have any more questions or bright ideas you'd like to share, J.W.?"

I got up. "No. I've shot my wad, I think. I'll go home and leave the detecting to you two. The kids and I have a rope bridge to build."

Dom frowned. "A rope bridge?"

"Like in *Tarzan and the Leopard Woman*," I said.

"Hey," exclaimed Olive, surprising me for the second time in five minutes, "I saw that movie when I was a kid! *Tarzan and the Leopard Woman*. Great! Johnny Weissmuller as Tarzan." She looked at Dom. "When I was a little girl I wanted to be Sheena. You remember Sheena? The female Tarzan? That looked like a good life to me, living there in a tree with Bob, wearing nothing but a leopard-skin bikini. Terrific!"

Dom studied us. "I've heard about Tarzan and I used to read about Sheena in the comic books, but I've never seen a movie about either one of them. Did I live a culturally deprived childhood?"

Olive and I found ourselves looking at each other and nodding. It was the first thing we'd agreed about in as long as I could remember.

"Yes, you did," I said.

"Yes, you did," echoed Olive.

I left the two of them to continue their discussion of crime and culture and went out to the Land Cruiser, where my children were playing Crazy Eights. Crazy Eights and Hearts are two great kid games: they last a long time and all you need is a deck of cards.

"Pa, are we going to work some more on the bridge now?"

"Yes, we are."

"Are you through talking with the police?"

"Yes, I am."

When we came out of the parking lot, I turned left, then left again onto Eastville Avenue, then right onto County Road. Somewhere near the old Tradewinds Airport I became aware of a car close behind me. I'm not the island's fastest driver, so having a car behind me wasn't unusual. This car, however, was too close, so I pulled to the right and slowed down so it could pass. But it didn't pass, and I speeded up again. So did the car.

I was very conscious of having my children with me. I tried using my rearview mirror but could see nothing of who was driving or how many people might be in the car. I speeded up even more and so did the car. I slowed down and so did the car.

Just before the intersection with the Edgartown-Vineyard Haven road is an entrance to the Jardin Mahoney garden center, which is always busy during the summer. I braked hard and turned in, hearing the angry squeal of brakes behind me before the car followed me. I slipped into a parking place between two cars where ladies with happy faces were loading plants into their trunks, jumped out, and watched the car slow and then drive on. Through an open window I saw an angry face and a clenched fist that became the bird, and heard a furious voice say, "Killer! We'll find you again!" And then the car was gone.

Although I was glad to spend the rest of the day working on the rope bridge, I had a hard time getting that face and fist out of my mind. It wasn't easy. I finally managed it by trying to imagine Olive Otero as Sheena. That wasn't easy either.

By the time Zee got home from work, we had finished building most of the platform in the oak tree. It was about six-by-eight and was supported partially by limbs and partially by struts attached to the trunk of the tree, and it had a space cut for the trapdoor that would lead down to the short rope walkway that led to the ground.

It was a good day's work, and the kids and I celebrated honest weariness with lemonade and oatmeal cookies.

Zee was impressed when Joshua and Diana led her out to show her the progress we had made, and we all basked in her praise. Indoors again, I poured big-people drinks and put nibblies on a plate and Zee and I went up to the balcony. Joshua and Diana, not to be outdone, climbed into the tree house with their food and drink.

I thought about the car that had followed me and was in no mood to make a complicated supper. Maybe pizza. It was too late to make my own, but I could order a couple and bring them home. My dry mouth moistened. Pizza, made right, is food for the gods. You could probably live a long, healthy life eating nothing but pizza.

I proposed my plan to Zee, who predictably thought it was a fine idea.

"You three did good work today," she said.

"A few more days and we should be done." I told her about Olive Otero being a Tarzan and Sheena fan.

"Well, well," said Zee. "Maybe the two of you can now stop scratching at each other's eyes and become pals, united by fantasies about Hollywood jungles. That would be nice. I'm sure that Dom would be greatly relieved."

I tried to imagine Olive and me as pals. Stranger things have probably happened, but I couldn't think of one.

"Speaking of Olive," said Zee, "guess who came into the ER today. Nathan Shelkrott, Wilma's husband."

"Who's Nathan Shelkrott and what's he got to do with Olive?"

Zee gave me a patient look. "He doesn't have anything to do with Olive, but Olive is a police officer and the police are investigating these Highsmith shootings, so when you mentioned Olive it reminded me of Nathan coming in, because Nathan and Wilma both work for the Highsmiths. She's the housekeeper and he does all of the outdoor work. I've known Wilma for years. I'm sure I've mentioned her name to you."

I remembered that Dom had mentioned a housekeeper. "What was Nathan doing in the ER?"

"He had chest pains, so Wilma drove him to the hospital. He's had a little heart trouble in the past and they were both worried. The tests didn't show anything, but they're keeping him for the night. They think he's just stressed out, which would be understandable. First Henry Highsmith and now his wife. What next? It's as though the whole Highsmith household is part of a Greek tragedy."

"How's your friend Wilma holding up?"

"She's worried." Zee sipped her drink. "But then, Wilma has looked worried for a long time. She has one of those troubled faces, but usually if you ask her what's the matter she always says it's nothing. This time, though, she didn't say that. She said it was getting to be too much for Nathan. First the Willet girl and now these shootings. I asked her what she meant, but she just shook her head and walked away."

I said, "Who's the Willet girl?"

"You remember," said Zee. "She's the girl who drowned at Great Rock."

"Ah, yes. Your friend Wilma didn't explain what she meant?"

"No."

"I have some odd news," I said, and I told her about the incident with the car.

"Maybe it was just road rage," I added. "There are a lot of crazy people around these days."

Zee didn't like that theory. "Do you think that's what it was?"

"Maybe."

"I think you should tell the police. Did you see the license plate?"

"No, I missed it."

"I don't think a road-rage person would have said what he said. I want you to call the police right now."

It was the advice I'd have given in her place. "Maybe you're right," I said, and I went down to the phone and talked to Dom Agganis.

"That's not much for us to go on," said Dom. "You be careful for the next few days. My guess is that somebody's decided that you're in the middle of this Highsmith business whether you think you are or not."

"I'll be careful," I said, and went back up to the balcony.

I sipped my drink and looked out over our garden. Beyond the barrier beach on the far side of the pond, white boats were moving over Nantucket Sound, heading for anchorages through the slanting light of late afternoon. I watched them cutting through the same sea that had drowned the Willet girl and thought of the ancient faith wherein beauty and death are part of the same cosmic dance.

12

Joanne Homlish, the woman who had supposedly seen me force Abigail Highsmith off the road, lived just off Tiah's Cove Road in a farmhouse that had been there since before the Revolution. It was not far from the home of Nancy Luce, the lonely, sickly "hen lady" poet whose body now lies in the West Tisbury graveyard, her stone and grave adorned with chicken statues placed there by her devotees. Nancy's poetry and other writings, her love of her cows and chickens, and her long, eccentric life had made her locally famous before her death in 1890, and now, more than one hundred years later, many a Vineyard living room wall sports a reproduction of a famous photo of Nancy seated in a chair, with her long, haunted face peering at the camera while her strong, gentle hands hold two of her beloved bantams.

It pleased me to think that not only Nancy, who had never traveled farther than Edgartown, was still remembered with affection, but that the same was true of her adored chickens—Beauty Linna, Bebbee Pinky, Tweedle Deedle, and the rest. What other chickens, aside from Chanticleer, have been immortalized by poetry? Maybe Nancy and Geoffrey were even now sitting together in some poet's heaven, discussing rhyme and open verse. I thought they'd probably have much to talk about.

Joanne Homlish's house was bigger than Nancy's

had been, and in spite of its years was well maintained in a neat yard behind which was an equally well kept old barn that now served as a garage, so evidenced by the middle-aged Ford Explorer that was parked inside its open door. Like everything else at Joanne's place, the Explorer looked to be in good shape. Only the some-times-yellow and sometimes-blue trim on lower windows of the house was unusual, since gray or white trim was the Vineyard norm.

"Are we there yet?" asked Diana, who with her brother was along for the ride because I, unlike most fictional sleuths, was a married man without a babysitter.

"I think we are," I said, stopping in front of the house. I cast a final look into my rearview mirror and still saw no following car.

"Can we get out of the truck?"

"Let's wait and see if there are dogs. Sometimes dogs don't like visitors, and I don't want you to get bitten."

We waited, but no dogs showed up. Maybe Joanne, like me, was a cat person.

"Stay here for the time being," I said.

I got out of the truck and knocked on the front door. A sharp-faced elderly woman opened it and looked at me and the truck. A pair of reading glasses hung on a cord around her neck.

"Mrs. Homlish? My name's Jackson."

She nodded. "What can I do for you, Mr. Jackson?"

"I want to talk to you about the bike accident you saw the other day."

"You an insurance agent? I already told the police what I saw. I can't tell you anything they don't already know."

"I'm not an insurance agent, but I have an interest in the accident and I'd like to know just what you saw."

"Well, all right." She peered over my shoulder.

"Those your children? They look about the age of my grandchildren. Let them get out and run around. No use making them sit there while we talk. They can't get hurt or do any damage."

When she smiled, her face became softer. I went to the truck and opened a door and the kids climbed out and looked around.

"Wander around all you want," Mrs. Homlish said to them, waving an arm that took in her whole property. "Just be careful." She looked at me. "Kids these days are kept on too short a leash, if you ask me. When I was a girl we didn't have seatbelts or crash helmets or any of that stuff, and we survived just fine. A kid has to get some scratches and bruises now and then, if you ask me."

"I like your style," I said, and told her about the tree house and the rope bridge.

She nodded approvingly. "My dad was no good with tools," she said, "so I never had a tree house. Wanted one, though. Instead, my brothers and I used to build forts in the barn made out of baled hay. We'd set up other bales on end and pretend they were attacking our castle and we'd shoot them with our bows and arrows and stab them with our bayonets. We had a couple of old World War One bayonets around the place and they made good swords. Nowadays kids can't even carry pocketknives to school. I think things have gone downhill. You want to stay out here so you can keep an eye on your kids, or do you want to talk inside?"

My children were already moving toward the barn, and I wondered what they'd do if they found bales of hay impaled with arrows and bayonets. I poked a thumb at the Land Cruiser and said, "I know this is an odd question, but have you ever seen this truck before?"

She looked at the truck with her bright old eyes.

"Seen some that look like that, more or less." Then her voice became angry. "Saw one the other day, in fact. Drove that Mrs. Highsmith right off the road, then just kept right on going! I'd have followed him and turned him in, but I stopped to help her. Say, that wasn't you, was it? You aren't up here to try to talk me out of what I saw, are you? You're wasting your time if you are!"

I held up a hand to stop the fire in her eyes from burning mine. "It wasn't me, but the description you gave the police and the picture of the truck you identified made them think it might have been me. I came here to find out if they got the story straight."

Her voice was hard as cast iron. "They got it straight, all right. It was a rusty old SUV just the shape and color of your machine right there. I doubt if there are many of them still on the road."

"This is the only one that I know of on the island. How long did you follow it before the accident?"

She knew exactly. "From the time I came out of Old County Road onto North Road. I had to stop so the truck could go by, headed for Vineyard Haven. I followed it until it ran Mrs. Highsmith off the road."

"So you got a good look at it."

"Yes, I did!"

"Good. You saw the front of the vehicle as it approached the intersection with Old County Road, and the side as it passed in front of you, then the back as you followed it toward Vineyard Haven. Is that right?"

She nodded, her eyes watchful now. "Yes, it is."

"Did you notice the driver as the SUV approached you and then passed the intersection in front of you?"

For the first time, she hesitated. Then she said, "No, I didn't, and I'm sorry I wasn't paying attention because then I'd know him when I see him again."

"The driver was a man, not a woman?"

She frowned. "Well, now that you mention it, I'm not really sure. But that was my impression, for some reason. I didn't pay much attention to the driver or to the SUV either, until just before the accident."

"Why then?"

"Because I could see Mrs. Highsmith on the bicycle up ahead of us and instead of slowing down—you know how twisty and narrow that road is—he speeded up. Damn fool! I thought, and I looked hard at the truck because I thought the driver should have his license taken away from him for reckless driving! And I was right too, because just as he was passing her, he swerved toward her and drove her off the road! She could have been killed!" She shook her head. "And now her husband's been murdered, they say. What more can happen to that family? And what about the rest of us, with a killer walking loose?"

It was pretty clear that she hadn't heard about Abigail Highsmith being shot, and I thought she should know. First, though, I said, "Will you walk out behind my truck and take a good look at it and tell me if it's like the one you saw?"

I glanced to my right and saw my children coming out of the barn, bearing neither arrows nor bayonets.

Joanne Homlish and I walked out and stood twenty feet behind the Land Cruiser. She studied the truck and nodded her head. "Yes. Same shape, same rust, same color. No doubt about it. Either this is the truck or it's got a twin."

I walked with her back to the house. "Do you remember the make of the SUV, or the license plate number?"

She shook her head. "I saw your license plate clear enough just now, but like I told the police, the license plate on the truck I followed looked as though it was splashed with mud, like the truck had gone through a mud puddle or something. And as far as the make of the truck goes, I have to admit I don't know one make from another these days. When I was growing up, I knew which ones were which because they all looked different; but nowadays they all look the same."

"I have the same problem." Joshua and Diana were walking toward us, so I lowered my voice and said, "The day before yesterday someone shot Abigail Highsmith. She's in a hospital in Boston. I haven't heard any reports about her condition today."

"Good heavens! I haven't been off the place for a couple of days so I hadn't heard. Do they know who did it?" She suddenly had a thought and looked hard at me.

"It wasn't me," I said, reading her mind. "The kids and I were building the rope bridge when it happened. But I thought you should know because whoever did it might be the person who drove Mrs. Highsmith into the ditch, and there's a chance he might find out that you saw the accident."

She paled slightly, then pulled herself together. "You mean he might try to intimidate me . . . or worse?"

"I doubt it, but it's possible. You should be a little more careful than usual."

"Than today, for instance?" Her smile was small and hard.

I hadn't thought of that. "Yes," I said. "Than today."

"My husband will be coming in from the east field for lunch. I'll give him the news. Meanwhile, I'll get his duck gun out of the closet."

"Do you know how to use a gun?"

"What do you think?"

She reminded me of one of those pioneer women

crossing the plains in a covered wagon. "I just wanted to be sure," I said.

"Pa."

I turned and looked down. "What, Diana?"

"Look. I found this in a nest and brought it here to the lady." She held up her little hand and showed us a brown egg.

"Why, thank you, honey," said Mrs. Homlish, taking the egg. "Did you see any others?"

"No, but we saw some hens and a rooster behind the barn."

"And we saw the pig in his pen," added Joshua.

Ham and eggs, I thought, but didn't say.

Joanne Homlish glanced at the sun. "Before you leave, maybe we should all have some cookies and cold milk. How does that sound?"

It sounded fine to Joshua and Diana, so we went in, and I saw that the house was as neat inside as out. Joanne Homlish liked things Bristol fashion. We sat around the table in her white kitchen and she gave us homemade chocolate chip cookies and cold glasses of milk. Delish.

After we had thanked her and said good-bye, and were driving away, Joshua said, "She's a nice lady, Pa. I didn't know she was a friend of ours."

"Pa."

"What, Diana?"

"Can we get some chickens?"

"I don't think so."

"How about a pig?"

"No. Definitely not a pig."

"Why not?"

"Because we don't live on a farm. You can have pigs and chickens if you live on a farm, but we don't."

"Let's buy one!"

"I don't have enough money to buy a farm."

"Can we have a dog? You don't have to live on a farm to have a dog."

I should have seen that coming, but I hadn't. "No. No dogs. You have a computer and we have cats. I don't want any dog."

"Because they're slaves and you don't approve of slaves?"

Joshua had clearly remembered my anti-dog argument, voiced whenever the subject of a dog had come up in the past.

"That's right."

"And because their owners are slaves too?"

It was the other half of my argument.

"Right again. Now that's the end of the dog talk."

"Pa."

"What?"

"Can we go to the beach?"

"Yes, we can, but I have to make one stop first."

The stop was at the West Tisbury police station, where I learned that Deputy Victoria Trumbull was not in, but was probably at home, gardening. I drove to her house, and there she was. Victoria, at ninety-two, was the oldest police deputy I had ever heard of. She was also sharp as a tack and seemed to remember everything she'd ever seen or heard during her long Vineyard life; certainly she knew more about the island than I would ever know. I asked her whether Joanne Homlish was an honest woman.

Victoria looked up at me with her ancient eyes, and a small smile lifted the corners of her mouth.

"You looking for a dishonest one, J.W.?"

"I might have done that when I was a lot younger, but not now."

"I'm glad to hear it. To answer your question, Joanne is straight as a gun barrel."

I thanked her, and the kids and I went home, changed into our swimming suits, and headed for the beach. On the way I wondered why honest Joanne was sticking to her story that the SUV that had driven Abigail Highsmith into the ditch looked just like mine, when I knew I'd never seen another such ancient Land Cruiser anywhere in my island travels.

Everywhere I drove I watched for following cars but saw only the normal kind.

— 13 —

I had been thinking about the Highsmiths' employees, Nathan and Wilma Shelkrott, and their visit to the hospital, so after we got home from the beach and had showered and changed into dry clothes, I drove with the kids back downtown to the library on North Water Street. It's a brick Carnegie library that has been expanded over the years.

It pleased me to know that in an age of computers the library still needed more space, and it pleased me still more to know that my children, in spite of the usefulness and pleasures of our computer at home, had, like me, a love of books that made a visit to a library a joy and a comfort. For there are few better feelings than to sit surrounded by books, knowing that you can never read them all no matter how hard you try. Ten thousand computer screens could never provide so warm a feeling.

And, of course, librarians are also book people who, unlike many public employees, actually like helping customers. In this case, the first one we met smiled at us and said, "Three Jacksons in a clump! To what do we owe this pleasure?"

"These two will want to have a look at the kids' books," I said, "and I want to look at some of your *Gazettes* and *Times*. The ones carrying the stories about the teenage girl who drowned up at Great Rock."

She looked at Joshua and Diana. "You know where to go."

They did and went there.

"You find a seat, J.W., and I'll find the papers."

I did and she did.

Vineyard papers don't like to dwell on the darker episodes of island life, preferring to emphasize stories that won't drive summer people away. Drownings, like moped and bicycle fatalities, are usually one-issue stories accompanied by warnings about riptides or untrained riders. Such was the case of the Willet drowning. I'd read the stories when they'd come out, but hadn't given them much attention, having only the feelings of sadness and repressed anger that usually attend the needless death of a young person who perishes because of carelessness or rashness. Now, though, I read the stories carefully.

Heather Willet had been fifteen years old and, being a prep school girl, had started her summer holiday on the island with her mother while public school students were still at their studies. A dozen prep school friends had been partying at the beach, and Heather and some others had gone for a swim as darkness fell. After a time her friends noticed that she was missing and had begun looking for her. The police had been called and about midnight her body had been found just off the rocky shore to the east, where the rising tide had carried it. The body had shown evidence of trauma consistent with contact with the rough shore, but death was due to drowning.

Her father, who worked in New Haven and normally joined his family only on weekends, had expressed outrage and grief and the hope that other young people would learn a lesson from the tragedy and never let friends swim alone or unattended. Her friends at the beach party, many of whom were fellow students at St. James Manor, were filled with sorrow. A girl named Tiffany Brown was quoted: Heather had

been carefree and full of life, a pretty and popular figure at St. James, a friend who would be greatly missed
and never forgotten. It was a view voiced by all others at
the party.

The police were circumspect but the reporters wrote
of evidence of drinking and possibly drugs at the party
site. The investigation of the accident would continue.

It was the sort of story that appeared regularly in
newspapers: an early-summer party gone bad. Had
Heather Willet not gone for that swim, or had a friend
been with her, there would have been no story. The
party participants would have gone home, sobered up,
and started planning the next good time.

I went through the stories again. The party hotline
was normally busy from June to Labor Day. Cell phones
made private parties into public ones and small parties
into giant ones. Loud music, alcohol, and chemical
additives were usual entertainments, and sensual pleasures were so common that a popular island joke held
that prostitutes couldn't make a living on the Vineyard
because there was so much free sex available, especially
during the summer.

But the beach party where Heather Willit had
drowned had been both small and private, perhaps
because it took place fairly early in the season, before a
lot of young people came to the island for sun, sand,
sex, and, perhaps, jobs.

I reread the lines suggesting the possible presence of
alcohol and drugs. Nothing specific was said, but the
inference was clear. No shock there, though, since only
the students and their parents might feign surprise at
such news.

There was no inference of sexual activity at the party.
Maybe the lovers, if there were any there, shared my
own view that a sandy crotch did little to encourage pas-

sion, the famous beach scene in *From Here to Eternity* notwithstanding.

On the other hand, youthful hormones being what they are, and beach blanket romance being a grand tradition, I wondered whether the evening swimmers had really all gone off to swim. There was no way to know from the articles.

Armed with the information in the stories, I thought about Nathan and Wilma Shelkrott. The stress that had sent Nathan Shelkrott to the hospital with heart problems was understandable considering the violence that had overtaken his employers, but Wilma Shelkrott had also tied Nathan's stress to the drowning of the Willet girl. Why?

I left my chair and found an island phone book. There were dozens of Browns. Too many for me to handle right now, but I could narrow the list later.

I went to the stacks and found the latest *Who's Who*. Just out of curiosity, I looked for my name. I was not there, as usual. But Jasper Jernigan was. I went back to my chair and read about him. The entry, like most, was brief, so, screwing my courage to the sticking point, I went to the library's computer, got on the Internet, and boldly punched in Jasper's name. Lo! a longer biography appeared. Joshua and Diana would be proud of their father!

There was no explanation about why Jasper's parents had given him such a name, but there was a good deal of information about Jasper himself. He had been born to a father who had done well in Florida real estate, and he had from childhood been enamored with golf. Since he could afford to play often, he did. After college he had begun building golf courses and had made a lot of money. Golf was his obsession and he was famous for his ambition to build bigger and better courses around the

world. He was a member of private clubs on five conti-
nents and on the board of many corporations. He had
married Helen Collins and was stepfather to her two
children, who attended the prestigious Tuttle School, of
which their mother was a graduate. The Jernigans'
principal residency was in Naples, Florida, but he also
had homes in Aspen, New York, Monterey, and on
Nantucket. His hobby was golf.

The biography understandably contained no reference to Jasper's enemies or to Gabe Fuller, and when I
looked for Gabe elsewhere on the Internet he, like me,
was not listed. I looked for the two Highsmiths and
they were there.

I wondered if Jasper and Henry Highsmith had ever
clashed other than in letters to the editors. Had they
ever wrestled in the fish market, for instance? Did
either of them even know what the other looked like?
Had some hired hand of Jasper's killed Henry to
weaken opposition to the boss's Pin Oaks proposal?
What had Dom Agganis learned when he interviewed
Jasper and Gabe?

Henry Highsmith had been on the faculty at Yale
and Abigail was at Brown. Both were tenured, both
had produced notable scholarly works, his in sociology
and hers in political science, and both held positions of
high esteem within the halls of ivy. Neither seemed
particularly controversial, but I recalled reading somewhere that academic politics could be ferocious precisely because the conflicts were so inconsequential, so
maybe Henry or Abigail had intellectual enemies furious enough to commit murder. If so, Dom Agganis
should be able to learn whether any of their angrier colleagues had been on the island when the Highsmiths
were attacked.

Henry's grandfather, Webster Highsmith, had boxed

at Harvard as an undergraduate and had been a member of the Olympic pentathlon team before going on to prosper in dry goods. Henry, like his male ancestors, had also studied at Harvard, where he took all three of his degrees and where he had met Abigail Hatter, descendant of a famous (to other people, not to me) line of scholars, who was doing the same. Before that, he had attended St. James Manor. Like his athletic grandfather he had excelled in sports, although, unlike Webster, not in the combative ones.

The Highsmiths lived in New Haven, with her commuting to Brown. They had two children, attended the Episcopal church, and were members of various academic, social, and liberal political organizations. They enjoyed tennis, skiing, sailing, and, of course, cycling.

Their photographs showed handsome, smiling faces.

I read the entries again and learned nothing more. I thought about what I knew and didn't know, got up and went to where Joshua and Diana were reading books, asked if they'd be okay if I left to talk with somebody for a little while, received assurances that they certainly would be, and walked to the offices of the *Vineyard Gazette* to find Susan Bancroft.

The *Gazette* is a justly famous newspaper that only prints stories pertinent to the island. There is general agreement that it wouldn't mention World War III except to report the enlistment of islanders and their subsequent return from abroad. It also makes little pretense of separating its editorial opinion from its news reporting. If you read a story about mopeds or proposals for golf courses or wind farms, you have no trouble knowing where the *Gazette* stands on the issue.

Susan Bancroft was the reporter who had written the story of Heather Willet's drowning. She was one of several Bancrofts who live on the Vineyard and a woman with whom, before I met Zee, I'd spent some quality time. In those days, she'd had another last name, but now she was a married woman. We were still on good terms in spite of our parting of ways.

I found her at her desk, pawing through a pile of papers, her specs balanced on the end of her nose.

"You look very reportorial," I said. "Like the beautiful lady correspondents in those old black-and-white movies about the newspaper biz."

"I start fussing around like this, trying to look busy, whenever somebody comes by," said Susan. "Just in case it's one of my bosses or a tattletale who wants my job. You don't want it, do you?"

"Not in a million years," I said. "Do you keep a bottle in your desk to celebrate scoops and breaking big stories?"

She peeked into a drawer and shook her head. "I guess not. Besides, scoops are pretty rare around here and the only big stories we handle don't break. They ooze on for months or years, so if I had one of those bottles it would last a lifetime. What brings you to this mecca of journalism?"

"You wrote the first story about the Willet girl who drowned up at Great Rock. You quoted a member of the beach party named Tiffany Brown. I don't know how to find her, but I'd like to talk with her."

She arched a brow. "What about?"

I hesitated between telling and not telling. "There may be nothing to it."

Her reporter's ears went up. "Is there a story here?"

"Not yet. Probably never."

If she'd been a dog, her nose would have been twitching. She waved at a chair piled with papers. "Put that stuff on the floor and sit down. Tell me what's going on."

I sat down. "Susan, I just want to talk with the girl."

"And so you shall. But I know you, J.W. You've got some reason to want to see her. What is it?" She snapped her fingers. "Say, this doesn't have anything to do with your finding Henry Highsmith's body, does it?"

"Why do you ask that?"

She counted the reasons on her fingers: "Because Henry Highsmith is dead, because his wife has been shot, and because their kids were both at the beach party when Heather Willet drowned. That last's the tie-in, isn't it?"

"You didn't mention the Highsmith children in your story," I said.

She made a dismissive gesture. "They weren't significant at the time." Then she leaned forward. "But maybe they are now that both of their parents have been shot. Why do you want to talk with Tiffany Brown?"

"I was going to ask her if the Highsmith kids were at the beach that night."

"I just told you that they were. So what if they were? What difference does that make?"

I made up my mind and I told her about Nathan Shelkrott going to the hospital and what Wilma had said to Zee. Susan listened without interruption. When I was through, we looked at each other. She had been a pretty girl when I'd dated her and was now a prettier woman. Her marriage had been as good for her as mine to Zee had been for me. She seemed more confident now, more certain of her thoughts and feelings.

"That's not a lot to go on," she said.

"No."

"It was a pretty casual statement, the way you tell it."

"Yes, but it impressed Zee enough for her to remember it."

"And it brought you here. Do you still want to talk with Tiffany Brown, or is it enough for me to tell you that Gregory and Belinda Highsmith were at the party?"

"I still want to talk with Tiffany. Something happened there that contributed to Nathan Shelkrott's tension and I'd like to know what it was. Maybe Tiffany can tell me."

"Why are you so interested?"

"Because some people believe I may have had something to do with what's happened to the Highsmiths, and I don't like it."

Susan studied me with wiser eyes than she'd had when we were an item, and said, "That's not the only reason, is it?"

"No." I told her about the incident with the car.

"Ah." She took off her glasses and tapped them lightly on her desk before she spoke. "It could be that Tiffany might not want to talk with a stranger," she said. "But she knows me. Suppose I make an appointment to see her and take you with me. You can be my assistant or something. I'll tell her that I'm working on a follow-up story and that I'm interviewing everyone who was there—the kids, the cops, everybody."

I thought about it for about ten seconds before I decided it was a good idea. "But I'm a little old to be your assistant," I said.

"Who, then?"

Inspiration struck. "Make me a writer who's interested in doing a book about the tragedy. That should loosen her tongue a bit."

Susan put on her glasses and studied me, then shook her head doubtfully. "You don't look like a writer."

I was hurt. "What does a writer look like?"

"Well, for one thing, they don't wear shorts and

T-shirts they get from the thrift shop. Well, maybe some of them do, but not many. Anyway, what we need isn't what writers actually look like, but what people think they look like. What Tiffany and probably her parents think they look like. You don't look like that."

"I have a polo shirt with a little animal over the pocket and I have some khaki pants. Will those duds do? I could be a writer down for the summer to write this book before I go back home to—where? Boston? New York? Fargo? Wherever writers live." Actually, I knew where a lot of them lived: they lived on Martha's Vineyard. Martha's Vineyard has more writers than Washington, D.C., has toadies.

"All right," said Susan. "I'll see if I can get us an appointment."

She dug a phone book out of a desk drawer, found the number, and called. She was a very smooth talker. When she hung up, she smiled and said, "I'll pick you up tomorrow morning. We'll take my car. I've seen yours."

— 14 —

That evening I made a kid-sitting deal with our neighbors the Nelsons, whose children and ours were friends, and left Joshua and Diana with them the next morning, with the understanding that I'd take their kids for the afternoon at our place. I wasn't home very long after delivering my children when Susan Bancroft's car came down our long sandy driveway. Susan and I had spent a few nights in the house during times past. It seemed long ago. She got out and looked around.

"You've spruced the place up a bit," she said.

"The civilizing influence of a good woman," I replied.

She smiled. "Are you implying that I wasn't a good woman?"

"You were good enough for me."

"Has the inside been spiffed up too?"

"The bedroom's neater."

Her smile became a grin. "I think we'd better let this dog lie right where it is. Come on. I'll take you to Chilmark."

"A good plan."

"When we get over the Chilmark line, keep your eye out for a driveway on the right," said Susan, as we pulled out of the yard. "One of the mailboxes is green."

We drove to West Tisbury and then took a right to the big oak and followed North Road toward Menemsha. On the way Susan asked me what I knew about the Browns.

"Only that Tiffany was a classmate of Heather Willet at St. James Manor. And I only know that because you said so in your article about the drowning. The Highsmith kids were St. James students too, and their father went there."

"What do you know about St. James?"

"Only that it's one of those premium prep schools that I can't afford, even if I wanted my kids to go there."

"They have scholarships, J.W. Your kids could probably qualify."

"I'm not deeply into prep schools, I'm afraid."

"Reverse snobbery is no better than the regular kind, J.W."

I ignored that remark and she went on to tell me that Tiffany's father was in stocks and bonds and her mother was in charitable activities, raising money from the wealthy for the poor. Their children, of whom Tiffany was the eldest, all attended St. James Manor and were on the Vineyard for the summer with their mother while their father, like many such in his economic class, joined the family for island weekends. During the off season, the Browns lived in West Haven, Connecticut, not far from where Dad kept the sloop he brought to the island every summer.

"I take it that Tiffany and her mother had no reservations about talking with you," I said.

A brief frown crossed her face, but she said, "I was nice to them the night of the drowning and I was nice to them on the phone, so they agreed to see me again. I didn't tell them I was bringing a photographer. That's you." She jabbed a thumb at a camera bag in the backseat. "There's an old SLR in there. I can show you how to use it."

"I can use a camera, but I thought I was going to be a writer."

She shook her head. "You don't look like a writer."

"I don't look like a photographer, either."

"Nobody looks like a photographer; not even photographers look like photographers, so it'll be okay. Just stand around and listen and take a lot of pictures. That's what photographers do: they take hundreds of pictures so they can get one good one."

"I want to find out why Nathan Shelkrott got so stressed by the drowning at the beach."

"Leave the questions to me. You just take pictures and keep your ears open."

There was something odd in her tone, and I turned in my seat and looked at her. "What's the problem, Susan? Something's bothering you about the interview. What is it?"

"Am I so transparent?"

"We knew each other pretty well a long time ago."

She nodded. "I remember. All right; the problem is that Tiffany isn't the sweetest kid I've ever met, and the same goes for some of the others who were there that night."

"They sounded innocent as lambs in your article."

"Do you actually know any innocent teenagers?"

"I know a few." Not too many, actually. I hadn't been a squeaky-clean teen myself, for that matter. I'd done things I still wouldn't tell my father if he were alive.

"You can judge Tiffany for yourself."

We crossed the town line into Chilmark, came to the green mailbox, and turned onto a narrow, bumpy dirt road. There are such roads all over Martha's Vineyard, leading off paved roads and winding through second- or third-growth forests and over hills that were bare of trees a hundred years earlier, when the island was covered with sheep and cattle pastures instead of summer houses. The roads are often kept bumpy to discourage unnecessary traffic and usually split up into even narrower branches leading first to this house and then the next and finally to the last of them, which nowadays, increasingly often, is a new palace with a view.

The Browns, according to a small, arrow-shaped sign, lived on the second branch of the main road. We went that way and came to the house, a big, rambling farmhouse with outbuildings in back, all of which were sided with weathered cedar shingles and sported gray-painted trim. It was classic Vineyard architecture. The lawns were cut and there was none of the clutter that so often spells poverty. Everything was almost too neat, like the pictures you see in magazines about fine living. To the south there was a distant view of the Atlantic, and to the west you could see Menemsha Pond, where, perhaps, Mr. Brown moored his boat during the summer. There was a flower garden on the sunny side of the house, with a white metal umbrella table and chairs in its center.

A woman and a teenage girl came out of the house. Both were wearing casual rich-girl clothes, old and comfortable but very pricey stuff. Both of them were blond and wore their hair fairly short. They looked almost like sisters until you looked again.

The woman put out her manicured hand. "How nice to see you again, Miss Bancroft."

The women shook hands and Susan gestured at me. "This is J. W. Jackson. He'll be taking photos, if you don't mind."

Barbara Brown looked at me and said coolly, "I didn't expect a photographer. I'd prefer it if no photographs were taken. This has been a trying time for us all." She placed a possessive hand on her daughter's shoulder and I saw the shoulder shrink.

I put a smile on my face and said, "Just as you wish, Mrs. Brown," and put my camera back in the case I'd slung over one shoulder.

"I remember you, Tiffany," said Susan. "We met at a terrible time for you, but you were very coherent and helpful in spite of the shock."

Tiffany looked wary. "I remember you too."

"As I told you on the phone," said Susan to Mrs. Brown, "I'm doing a follow-up story about the tragedy. I want to explore the after-effects of such an event. I plan to talk with the people at the beach party and with their families. I know it may be hard for Tiffany, but she was the most mature student I spoke to that night and her thoughts and feelings will be important in my story."

"I have coffee in the kitchen," said Barbara Brown, with the smile she no doubt used to extract charity money from the pockets of wealthy philanthropists. "Why don't I bring some out and we can sit in the garden while you do your interview? Tiffany, why don't you show Susan the way? Mr. Jackson, I do hope I haven't offended you. If you'll leave your equipment in your car, I'll be pleased to have you join us for coffee."

The mother walked into the house and the daughter led Susan to the garden table. I took the camera bag to Susan's car, tossed it into the backseat, and went up to the garden. There was so much fraud in the air that I felt like I was walking through a cloud.

Barbara Brown set the coffee tray on the table between herself and her daughter, and poured three cups. No coffee for Tiffany. I took mine black and made sure my chair was a bit outside the circle of women.

Susan, I thought, was up against two people who didn't want to tell her anything that might reflect badly on them. In that respect they were like most people who were often in the spotlight. The rest of us can get away with sometimes foolish speech or acts because no one pays much attention to what we say or do, but the rich and famous cannot because their faux pas can be headline news.

I didn't know how famous or rich the Browns really were, but Barbara Brown was clearly conscious of her social position and wasn't about to stray far from her daughter's side when a reporter was around. My impression was that Tiffany would have preferred Mom to be elsewhere.

Susan, however, was apparently used to such people and began her interview with more flattery about Tiffany's maturity before easing on to nonthreatening ground: Tiffany's memory of the earlier, happier portions of the beach party. No questions were asked about drugs, alcohol or, sex, and no information was volunteered.

A small, possibly cynical smile touched Tiffany's lips as she described the fire and the hamburgers and hot dogs and chips and the music and the dancing and the early swimming. Just a bunch of teenage friends having a good time together.

No, they hadn't all gotten there at the same time. Some had arrived a bit later. Greg and Belinda High- smith were the last arrivals. Tiffany's lips began to form a word, but she never spoke it. Her eyes shone.

Yes, she said to Susan, most of them attended St. James Manor, but a few were from other schools: Bitsy Evans was from Inverness, and Margy Collins and her brother Biff, Greg's best friend, were from Tuttle and had come from Nantucket just for the party. There had been, let's see, fourteen of them in all. They and their parents had met over the years and all were friends or acquaintances. There were no new kids there.

Barbara Brown sipped her coffee and emphasized the closeness of the participants and their families. All very good families, very good. Everyone had been devastated by Heather Willet's death.

Susan could well understand that and their consternation at how such a tragedy could have happened.

Tiffany opened her mouth but it was Barbara who spoke, explaining that as it was getting dark, four of the kids went off for a final swim. Who were the four? Why, poor Heather, of course, and Belinda and Greg (those two poor dears are never far apart, are they, Tiffany?), and Biff Collins. Isn't that right, Tiffany?

Yes, Mother.

Yes, and Biff is the captain of his swimming team and is going to be lifeguarding at Nantucket this summer, and he swam way out into the sound and came back and found Belinda and Greg running up and down the beach and calling for Heather. Isn't that right, Tiffany?

Yes, Mother.

And then everybody was looking and Margy Collins called 911 on her cell phone and when the police and divers and the others finally got there they eventually found poor Heather off to the east by the rocks. It was almost midnight and it was all just terrible. Poor Tiffany and the others were so brave and Barbara was proud of them all, but it was an awful shock to everyone.

"And how have the survivors coped since then? Have there been any changes in thoughts or feelings about life?"

"Well," said Barbara, "there was absolutely no question but that the children had taken a new look at life. It was like they had been thrust suddenly into adulthood, into a more mature understanding of things. They were still children, of course, but they were more thoughtful, more . . . more grown up and serious."

Tiffany said that everyone had gone to the funeral back in Connecticut and that Heather's parents had been devastated and that the kids had felt just terrible but hadn't had much to say at first but now they were getting back together again, though things weren't the same, you know?

"It's been a weird summer," she said, gesturing and knocking over the coffeepot. The coffee spilled on her mother's thigh and Barbara gave a little scream and pushed away from the table and brushed furiously at her slacks.

"Damn! Look what you've done!" She caught her anger before it came out more strongly. "Please be more careful, dear! Oh, what a mess! Please excuse me. I'll have to change." She rose and tried a laugh. "Well, accidents do happen in the best of families. I'll bring more coffee. No, please don't get up. I'm fine. Just stay right there."

She glared at Tiffany and went into the house.

I looked at Tiffany. "She's gone," I said.

Tiffany looked at Susan. Her face was twisted. "I hate her! She's such a phony! They're all phonies! You know why Greg and Belinda were late? Because they had to sneak out of their house. Their parents didn't want them going to parties! And you know why Heather went swimming with them and Biff? Because she had the hots for Greg, that's why! She was naked when they found her. Did the cops tell you that? I bet they didn't!"

Susan stared at her and the girl gave a laugh that sounded like the bark of a dog.

"Tell me about Heather," I said.

"She was a bitch in heat," said Tiffany. "I don't miss her, and neither does anyone else!"

"Who brought the booze and dope?" I asked.

Tiffany gave me a look of contempt. "It was BYO, as usual. You use it, you bring it."

"Do you all have a dealer?"

She studied me. "I'm going to deny all of this, you know. If they put my hand on the Bible, I'll still deny it."

"Fine. Do you have a dealer?"

She looked at the doorway through which her mother had gone. "I get what I need from my friends. I don't need a dealer."

"How about an obstetrician or a gynecologist?"

"No, but they're not hard to find."

The house door opened and Barbara Brown came out, bringing more coffee.

Tiffany closed her mouth. Susan scribbled on her notepad. I accepted another cup of black coffee. As I sipped it and Barbara Brown spoke to Susan, commenting about how the tragedy had brought everyone closer together and had sensitized them to the real values in life, I caught Tiffany's eye and she gave me a smile that was so cynical that I could have choked on it when I swallowed.

— 15 —

"Well," said Susan, as we drove away. "Quite a show, I'd say."

"A lot of kids that age are mad at their parents."

"The girl seemed just as bitter about her friends, if you can call them that."

I thought of the motive that had brought me here and said, "When I get mad it's usually because some part of my world seems in danger."

"The wit and wisdom of Psych 101," said Susan. "Well, did you learn what you wanted to learn?"

"Maybe. If we can believe Tiffany, the Highsmith kids sneaked out of the house that night and the Willett girl not only wanted sex with Greg but lost her bathing suit while she was off with him and the other two kids. Maybe his knowledge of that was what put Nathan Shelkrott in the hospital. Did you know she was naked when they found her? It wasn't in your story."

She nodded. "I knew about it and I saw the beer cans and vodka bottles, but I couldn't be sure about sex and drugs so I didn't write about them. I haven't seen the final autopsy report, so I don't know what it says, but unless the police decide to arrest somebody for something, I doubt if it would be much of a story even then."

"You could write it using what Tiffany said just now."

She shook her head. "I need collaboration. I can't use the accusations of one upset teenager who'll deny everything under oath. I need to talk with more people."

"The kids have had time to agree on a story."

"Yes, but Tiffany spilled the beans and some of the others may, too, whether or not they've all agreed to tell the same tale. I'll see as many of them as I can, using the same follow-up-story ploy I used with the Browns. Now, though, I can use Tiffany's little tantrum to maybe pry out some information I couldn't have gotten before."

"You still need a photographer?"

"It'll take me a while to set up more interviews, and this time I'll ask if I can bring a cameraman along. If anybody says it's okay, you're welcome to join me."

Susan dropped me off at our house and I looked at my watch. It was the good $9.99 kind that did everything it was supposed to do and was cheap enough so you didn't have to go into mourning if you broke or lost it. No one should ever pay more than $9.99 for a watch, but a lot of people do. Mine told me that I still had some time before I had to pick up Joshua and Diana and the Nelson kids.

I drove to the hospital and nobody followed me. Zee spoke before I could even open my mouth.

"I finally have some good news for you," she said. "Mattie and I and all our kids are going on a shopping trip to New Bedford in a few days and we're not taking our husbands."

"Are you leaving your credit card at home?"

"Absolutely not. I'm just leaving you."

"Thanks for that, at least. I don't suppose you know where Nathan Shelkrott is."

Zee picked up a pile of papers. I tried but failed to read them upside down. "When he left here," she said, "Nathan was headed for home."

Home was the Highsmith place, I guessed, up on Middle Road in Chilmark. Whatever Henry Highsmith's other qualities might have been, he had good taste in real estate. Middle Road is about as pretty a road as you can find on Martha's Vineyard and Chilmark is its prettiest township.

"You're snooping," said Zee, sounding neither surprised nor enthusiastic. "It's because of that car business, isn't it?"

"I'd like to know who was in it. Has anybody followed you?"

"Not that I know of. I'm sure that both the police and I would be happier if you left the detecting to them."

"If you notice anybody following you, I want you to drive to a police station without stopping."

She put a hand on my arm. "All right, but I don't want you to worry about me. What happened this morning?"

"I may have learned some things that the police don't know." I told her about Tiffany and her mother, then asked, "Did you know that Heather Willet was naked when they found her body?"

She nodded. "I was on duty when they brought her here."

All of the dead bodies on the Vineyard are brought to the hospital before traveling on to the medical examiner or to funeral homes.

"Did you think there was anything significant about the body being naked?"

"No, because skinny-dipping isn't a lost art." She paused. "And neither is teenage sex."

"Did you see any indication that she might have had sex?"

"I didn't make a thorough examination. Besides, she'd been in the water for hours and water is an effective cleanser. For what it's worth, the ME didn't find any indication that the girl had had any recent sex."

I didn't know whether or not to be surprised. "Recent?"

She shrugged. "She wasn't a virgin."

"I didn't read about that in the papers."

"It wasn't in the papers. Probably out of respect for the family. The girl was dead, after all, so what difference did it make?"

None, probably. I wondered if Mommy and Daddy had known about their little girl's private life. How old had Heather been? Fifteen?

"What did you make of the contusions and abrasions on the body?"

Zee looked up at me. "You're awfully interested in Heather Willet all of a sudden."

"Humor me."

She went back to her papers. "Like I said, I didn't do a thorough examination, but the bruises on her head looked consistent with a fall against a hard object. They found the body in the water just outside those rocks on the east end of the beach, remember, and if she'd been drinking . . ."

"Had she?"

"The ME said yes, although I don't think the girl was officially drunk. Anyway, I thought it was possible that she'd been drinking and had wandered away from the other kids and had fallen and hit her head on a rock and drowned. The abrasions looked consistent with damage caused by the body being tumbled against rocks. The ME came to the same conclusion."

"No sign of foul play."

"What's that supposed to mean? What's Henry Highsmith's death got to do with Heather Willet? You should keep your focus." She gave me a worried look, such as wives give when their husbands go through midlife crises.

"My focus is just fine," I said. "Here's what we have so far: First, Henry Highsmith tries to start a fight with me in the fish shop for no good reason and then he and his wife both get themselves shot. Then some guys in a car follow me and call me a killer. Today I learn that the two Highsmith kids sneaked out of their house a couple of weeks earlier to attend a beach party where, according to Tiffany Brown, Heather Willet, who has the hots for the Highsmith boy, goes off with him and his sister and another kid and ends up naked and dead. You tell me that Wilma Shelkrott brought her husband to the hospital because she was afraid he was having a heart attack brought on by the party. That's two deaths and two hospitalizations involving the Highsmiths. I'd like to know why Nathan Shelkrott panicked because of the beach party."

She spread her hands. "Maybe he felt responsible somehow. Maybe the parents left the Shelkrotts in charge of the kids, and the kids escaped and ended up in the middle of a party where booze and drugs were involved and a friend drowned. Maybe he was afraid he and his wife would get fired."

"How long have the Shelkrotts worked for the Highsmiths?"

"I don't know," said Zee, going back to her papers. "Years."

"Didn't you tell me that Wilma Shelkrott has been worried for a long time? What's she been worried about?"

"How should I know? Maybe she and her husband have been worried about getting fired and they were afraid the beach party would be the excuse the Highsmiths needed. Or," said Zee, "maybe Wilma's just a worrywart."

"Or maybe she's just one of those people who looks worried but really isn't."

"Maybe," said Zee, "but I don't think so."

I trusted Zee's instincts about Wilma. Full-time fretters are often what I call baroque worriers. Baroque worriers worry in complex, highly convoluted ways about unlikely things that would never occur to most people, and that often depend on a whole series of equally unlikely things happening first. The form and content of their worries are often wonderfully ornamented, like a composition by Bach, and like much of Bach's work they take a lot of time to complete; thus baroque worriers are inclined to worry most of their waking hours, unlike classic worriers, who get through their worries much more quickly and have time left to do other things.

I try not to worry about anything. Although I'm not actually able to do that, the effort itself annoys some hard-worrying people, who view it as a kind of insult to humanity. They may have a point, because not only are people probably the only animals who worry, they're probably the only ones who should.

"Any news about Abigail Highsmith?" I asked.

"I hear that she's stable. I think her sister is up in Boston with her."

I thought back. "I heard that an uncle is here on the island looking after the kids, and that an aunt is with Abigail."

Zee finished sorting papers and putting them into separate stacks, and began to put the different piles into different files, thus offering yet more evidence of the false prophecy that paperwork would end forever when computers entered the mainstream of human enterprise. As every clerk or public servant knows, there's more paperwork now than before.

"And Wilma and Nathan are up there at the house with Unc and the kids," I said. "Do the Shelkrotts live right there in the main house or do they have a place of their own?"

"I think they have what used to be called the servants' quarters."

She was only half joking. Of the dozens of gigantic new houses being built all over the island, many included servants' quarters that were elegant in both design and construction. According to a carpenter friend who was making excellent money working on the new castles, there was even a kind of competition among millionaires having to do with who was erecting the most gracious quarters for their maids and manservants. Our friend had taken me and Zee on a tour of his current project and indeed the servants' quarters, in that house at least, were lovely. Not, of course, as lovely as the main house, which, like many of its kin, was gigantic enough to host three generations of the family and sported hand-carved imported woods, Italian marble, and gold bathroom fixtures.

"Do you know the uncle's name, by any chance?"

She tapped the edges of a stack of papers to make a neater bundle. "His name is Brundy, or something like that. He's Abigail's brother-in law. The gossip is that the kids wanted to go to Boston to be near their mother but the adults thought it would be better if they stayed here. I think it was probably a good decision. All they could do up there is sit in a waiting room. Hospitals really aren't very well prepared to care for the children of hospitalized adults." She put the neat pile of papers into a file and slid the cabinet door shut. "You're going to the Highsmith house, I presume."

"I'd like to see Nathan Shelkrott, at least. Maybe Wilma too." I looked at my watch. "But not today. Today I have other obligations."

"What? To go fishing?" She feigned a pout. "It's not

fair, you know, to go fishing when I have to work! A real gentleman would never think of such a thing."

"I'm going to babysit the Nelson kids with Joshua and Diana. If all goes well, I'll get some more work done on the rope bridge."

"You'll need six eyes," said Zee. "One for each kid and the regular two for your work. Say, why not show the *Leopard Woman* movie again? Kids love to see the same movies over and over, and they may get an even better appreciation of the significance of the work you're doing."

I put my big hands on her shoulders and kissed her forehead. "You have an excellent mind," I said.

"I try to be of assistance," said Zee, "but you're not always easy to help. Happy babysitting."

No one followed me home.

16

Naturally, the Nelson kids loved *Tarzan and the Leopard Woman,* and naturally, my own kids loved it even more than before, and after watching it on our tiny black-and-white TV screen all four of them were more enthusiastic than ever about the tree house and the rope bridge and tried to be of help to me, the master carpenter, as I continued to work on the bridge after they'd seen the movie. Unlike Tarzan, Boy, and Jane, who had to do their building with whatever materials the jungle had to offer, I had electricity and modern tools, rope instead of vines, and other modern advantages, so I actually made some progress.

David McCullough, the island's finest writer, had once penned an excellent book on the building of the Brooklyn Bridge; it occurred to me that maybe he'd like to write one about our bridge, when we finished it, and I considered arranging for him to see *Tarzan and the Leopard Woman* as cultural preparation. I had never actually met David, but I knew he'd be a fan.

That evening, as Zee and I were sitting on our balcony, our backs to the slanting summer sun, I pointed out the day's progress and asked Zee what she thought of my idea about inviting David to win another Pulitzer by writing about our bridge.

"An excellent plan," said Zee. "I'm sure David will love it. He's probably been wondering what to do next."

There is no greater blessing than an agreeable wife. I

looked at Oliver Underfoot and Velcro, who were sociably sitting on the balcony railing, staring at nothing in catish fashion. "What do you two think?"

They too thought it was a fine plan. That made it unanimous.

The next day I put the kids in the Land Cruiser and drove to Chilmark. The Highsmith place was on Middle Road, but I wasn't sure exactly where, so I went first to the Chilmark police station for directions.

My route took me through West Tisbury, where we passed David McCullough's house. I decided not to stop and suggest the new bridge book, but instead went on to the Panhandle, then left on Middle Road, where, after the kids and I admired the big-horned oxen who welcome down-islanders to Chilmark, I checked mailboxes all the way to Beetlebung Corner but saw nothing that identified the Highsmith house. I did, however, see a box with the name Willet. Behind it, up the hill, the house and barn had an unoccupied look, and I remembered that after their daughter's death the surviving Willets had returned to the mainland.

The peripatetic Chilmark Police Department is locally famous for having its station moved from one location to another and then to another. I caught up with it at its latest address in what was once the old Menemsha School. The young officer unfolded a map and showed me that the Highsmith place was in fact next door to the Willet place, on an old road that had originally led up to a now long-abandoned stone quarry. Wouldn't you know?

The policeman put his finger on the quarry and waxed nostalgic: "It's been full of water as long as I can remember. We used to sneak up there and try to dive to the bottom but we never could get down that far. Some of the crazies drove an old jalopy in there once, and we never could dive deep enough to find it either. Last time I was up there, years ago, they had No Trespassing and No Swimming signs all around it, and now it's part of the Highsmith place so you can't get there anyway. I tell you, things have gone downhill since I was a kid. Nowadays half the island is forbidden territory."

I thought he was pretty young to be so wistful about the golden past, when every gate had been open and you could go anywhere, but maybe time passes faster these days.

I didn't tell him why I wanted to find the Highsmith place because I'm sometimes as covetous about information as anyone else. What is it that pleases us so much when we know something other people don't know? Is it a feeling of power? Sooner or later, of course, people with secrets almost always reveal them to someone, which is a good thing for the police, who have cuffed many a perp who couldn't keep his mouth shut about his crime and was ratted out by his listener.

After agreeing with Diana that we should seriously consider stopping at The Bite for a fried clam lunch, I drove back along Middle Road until I passed the Willet mailbox and came to a driveway leading up the hill to my left. The Highsmith mailbox had only a number on it, which explained why I had ignorantly passed it on my first trip. The driveway wound up through oak and underbrush to a grassy clearing on the hillside. Midway in the clearing was a large, newish house with an attached three-car garage, and beyond the house was the untended grassy remains of the road that presumably led on up to the old stone quarry.

There was an apartment over the garage where, I guessed, the Shelkrotts probably lived. The driveway circled in front of the garage and looped back onto itself. Looking to the south over the falling hillside, the house's occupants had a panoramic view of southern Chilmark and of the ocean, which curved over the horizon and next touched land at Hispaniola, homeland of Pedro Martinez and many other baseball notables. Aspiring Major Leaguers in the United States should learn what the Dominicans eat and make that their diet.

There was a Volvo sedan with New York plates parked in front of the garage beside a middle-aged blue Chevy station wagon with Connecticut plates. I parked next to them, speculating that the Volvo belonged to the visiting uncle and the Chevy belonged to the Shelkrotts.

"You kids stay out here," I said as we climbed out of the truck after I'd checked for dogs. "Don't go far. I have to talk with some people here."

"Can we walk around behind the garage?"

"Sure."

As I approached the house I could see a garden behind the garage. There wasn't much growing there yet, which suggested that it had been planted late, if at all. Everything in sight was neat and well maintained, but the place had an odd feeling that made me somehow uneasy, as though I were entering the world of the Fisher King.

A woman opened the door in answer to my knock. She had a faintly worried look on her face that made her look older than I guessed she was.

"Mrs. Shelkrott?"

"Yes?"

"My name is Jackson. I've just come from the Chilmark police station, and before that I was conferring with Sergeant Agganis of the state police about the shootings of Mr. and Mrs. Highsmith. I hope you don't mind me bringing my children. They're good about not disturbing things."

She looked at them as they walked toward the garden.

"I don't mind."

"I don't want to intrude," I said, "but as you know, the police often interview people more than once during their investigations. Do you and your husband have time to answer a few questions?"

"Conferring" was a stretch, but otherwise my tongue was only slightly forked. Wilma Shelkrott was only partly skeptical.

"Are you a police officer?"

I patted my hip and smiled. "I have a badge, if you'd like to see it."

That was true. It was my old Boston PD shield, long withdrawn from service.

I was pleased when she waved a hand and stepped aside. "Oh, no, that won't be necessary. Please come in."

I walked past her into an entrance hall with doors leading into three other rooms and a stairway leading up to a second floor. There was a coat closet beside a short deacon's bench and a bust of Socrates over a bookcase filled with leather-bound volumes that looked more decorative than utilized. I don't know many readers who bother to bind their books in leather; they tend to buy cheaper editions so when they wear them out they can afford new copies.

"Is your husband home?" I asked. "I want to talk with him too."

She seemed to want to wring her hands, but didn't. "I believe he's in the garage. I'll call him."

I shook my head and held my smile. "Before you do that, perhaps I can have a few words with you, if you don't mind."

Her eyes were unhappy. "I can't imagine how I can help you. All I can tell you is what I told the other officers who were here."

I tried to seem comforting. "Sometimes when we go over information again we get a detail that we overlooked before." I pulled a ballpoint pen and small notebook from my pocket, and flipped through a few pages. "Now, just to review the facts, how long have you and your husband been working for the Highsmiths and what duties have you performed for them?"

Wilma Shelkrott had answered that one before, and had no trouble repeating herself. They had come to work for the two Doctors Highsmith shortly after Mrs. Highsmith had given birth to Gregory, sixteen years before, and the young parents had realized that they would need help if they were both to progress in their academic careers, particularly since Abigail Highsmith had a long commute from New Haven to Providence, where she aspired to promotion at Brown.

Wilma attended to housework and child care, and Nathan cared for the house and grounds and the automobiles, and opened and closed the summer house before and after the season. She and her husband had, she said, always had excellent relations with the parents. What happened to the Highsmiths was terrible, simply terrible!

"How are the children doing?" I asked.

The furrows in her forehead deepened. "Their uncle Tom Brundy is with them here while his wife—that's Mrs. Highsmith's sister—is up in Boston with Mrs. Highsmith."

"How is Mrs. Highsmith?"

"We haven't heard since last night. There were no changes. Mrs. Brundy calls every evening to give us the latest developments."

"It must be hard on everyone."

"Yes."

I flipped a few pages, and looked at a new one. "I understand that your husband was recently hospitalized overnight. We're told you thought he might be having a heart attack but that his symptoms turned out to have been caused by stress. You've said that you and your husband had excellent relations with the Highsmiths; can you tell me what caused him so much anxiety?"

Her eyes held mine. "I'm afraid I really don't know."

I looked back at her. "I think you may know more than you're telling me. At the hospital you mentioned the swimming accident at the beach. Why would your husband have been so disturbed about that? The Highsmith children were safe, after all."

She shook her head. "I don't know what I meant. The accident had just happened and everyone was disturbed and shocked."

"You knew the girl who drowned?"

She hesitated. "Why do you ask that?"

"She lived next door. She was about the same age as Belinda Highsmith. The children surely knew one another as summer neighbors."

"Yes, I knew who she was. When they were younger, she used to come over to play with Gregory and Belinda once in a while." She paused and rubbed her chin. Her eyes seemed to focus elsewhere. "Not so much the last couple of years."

"They were at the beach party together. The Willet girl had gone off with Belinda and Gregory and another boy when she drowned."

"Yes, I heard about that. I can't tell you anything about it. I know they weren't close friends anymore."

"Tell me about Gregory and Belinda."

"What do you mean?"

"I mean what kind of kids are they? Do you get along with them? What are they like?"

She lifted her chin. "I took care of them from the time they were babies, but now they don't ask for my advice. I'm no psychologist, so don't ask me to analyze them. They're very close, I can tell you that."

"They sneaked out of this house to attend the beach party."

She stared. "Where did you hear that?"

"From one of their friends. Is it true?"

She took a deep breath. "Yes. Their parents were at a party and Nathan and I were in the house. Gregory and Belinda got out of a back window. We never knew they were gone until the police brought them home."

"Could that have caused your husband to have an anxiety attack? Were the two of you afraid that the Highsmiths would hold you responsible for their children having escaped from your care?"

"No. No, they didn't blame us. They knew how their children could be."

"How was that? How could they be?"

"You know: rebellious, wild, holding nothing sacred. Like teenagers are these days. Not like when I was their age."

It was a complaint that had probably been voiced by older generations since caveman days.

I stared at her. "But you said at the hospital that your husband's condition might have been triggered by the beach party. If he wasn't stressed by fear of being reprimanded, what was it that caused his chest pains?"

She rubbed that furrowed brow. "It was just the kids. You know, just the kids doing God knows what down on the beach and the Willet girl dying because they were crazy and didn't care what happened as long as it happened to somebody else. Nathan couldn't stand it."

I studied her. "And now," I said, "someone has murdered Henry Highsmith and has tried to murder Abigail Highsmith. How does Nathan feel about that? How do you feel?"

She had the look of a dead woman. "I feel like the world is ending, and so does Nathan."

I hardened my voice. "Do you know anyone who hates the Highsmiths enough to murder them?"

Her voice came out of her mouth like a wind from a cold cave. "There's evil in the world. It's everywhere. No one is safe. No one can explain it. No one knows where it will come from next. Nothing makes any sense. I don't understand anything anymore."

She turned away and walked out of the room.

I watched her until she was out of sight, then went outside and to the garage. I thought I heard my children's voices off to the west. They seemed to be agreeing that they'd found a trail. I hoped they wouldn't follow it.

There was a doorway beside the three closed garage doors. I entered and found myself at the foot of a stairway leading up to what I took to be an apartment. To my left was a door leading into the garages. I went through it and found myself in a woodworking area. A man was standing at a bench, painting fence pickets. He turned as I came in.

"Mr. Shelkrott?"

"Yes."

"I'm investigating the Highsmith shootings. I've just talked with your wife and now I'd like to talk with you."

A curtain seemed to fall over his face.

17

Nathan Shelkrott was a solid-looking man whom I judged to be in his sixties. He was balding and round-shouldered and was wearing a paint-spattered apron over a neat khaki shirt and trousers. His initial smile had been replaced by an expressionless mask.

"I know other investigators have been here already," I said, trying to sound friendly, "but it's routine for people like me to come around again just in case we missed something the first time. I hope you won't mind telling me some of the things you've probably said before."

He shook his head and put down his paintbrush. "I don't mind."

I thought that he probably did. "Fine," I said. "First, do you have any idea about who might want to harm the Highsmiths? It's rare to have two members of a family attacked at different times and in different places."

He ran his tongue over his lips. "Like I told the other policemen, I don't know anybody like that. The Highsmiths didn't have any enemies."

His eyes looked a bit too intently into mine.

"What can you tell me about Mr. and Mrs. Brundy? Was there any tension between them and the Highsmiths?"

"No! What a question! Mrs. Brundy is Mrs. Highsmith's sister! Mr. Brundy is out walking with young

Gregory and Belinda right now, and Mrs. Brundy is in Boston with Mrs. Highsmith."

"Do you know the Brundys well?"

His gestured with an open hand. "Not really well, maybe, but for many years. The Brundys often join us for holidays. They're on the best of terms with Henry and Abigail." He added with what seemed real anger, "I resent these questions. Why do you ask them?"

"Murder is often committed by the victim's associates, family, or friends," I said. "Are you sure there was no bad blood between the Highsmiths and the Brundys?"

"I'm absolutely sure!" He fumbled a blue-checked kerchief out of a back pocket and wiped his forehead.

The gesture inspired me to say, "People like you and your wife, who've worked for a long time for a family, know a lot about what goes on in the household. I think you may know more than perhaps you realize you know."

"You're not being clever," snapped Shelkrott. "I know the saying that no man is a hero to his valet. That's what you're implying, isn't it? That the Highsmiths must have done something to bring about these shootings, and that I know what it is. Well, I don't! They didn't deserve this; they didn't!"

I pushed harder. "After the Willet girl drowned, your wife thought you might be having a heart attack and took you to the hospital. What disturbed you so much?"

He looked away, then back at me. "It was a terrible night. A young girl was dead."

"And Gregory and Belinda had sneaked out of the house while you were supposed to be watching them, and they were at the beach when it happened."

"Yes. And it was my fault. I'd let them trick me. I was terribly stressed."

"Were you angry?"

"Of course I was angry."

"At Gregory and Belinda?"

"Yes, yes, of course! But more at myself for letting them sneak out like that!"

"Do they make a habit of breaking rules?"

He became careful. "They're teenagers. All teenagers break rules."

"Were you afraid you might lose your job?"

He was suddenly more at ease. "Of course not. Henry and Abigail knew how clever and willful their children could be. They didn't blame Wilma and me for what happened. It could have happened if they'd been home themselves. They'd already decided to send Belinda to school in Geneva this fall because they thought it would be good for both children if they were apart for a year and learned more self-discipline."

I changed tack. "Did you ever hear anything about the Highsmiths having problems with someone where they worked?"

He shook his head. "The Highsmiths were involved very deeply in their work at their universities, and they took it seriously; but they usually laughed about the academic feuds and arguments."

"Is it possible that some other professor might not have been so amused, but might have been really angry instead?"

He shook his head. "If so, I never heard about it. Besides, Brown and Yale are a long way from Martha's Vineyard."

True. A murderous professor would have had to come to the island, kill Henry and bury him, then hang around several days to shoot Abigail, all without drawing attention to himself. Such a scenario seemed unlikely, but I imagined that Agganis was checking it out. I rarely thought of possibilities that Dom hadn't considered.

I changed course again. "Tell me about the Willets. Did they socialize with the Highsmiths? They live next door and their daughter palled around with the Highsmith kids."

The mask that had hidden his face when I'd first come in hid it again. "The Willets haven't been back since their daughter's funeral in Connecticut."

"Yes. I'm told they're still away. Before that, though, they'd been neighbors of the Highsmiths for years, hadn't they?"

"Yes."

"Were they and the Highsmiths friends?"

"I suppose."

I felt a frown on my face. "You seem doubtful."

He took a breath. "Not at all. Yes, they were friends. Their children were about the same ages and they shared the problems of young parents."

"And the joys?"

"Yes," he said, "I suppose so." Then he added, "I don't know too much about children. My wife and I have none of our own."

"But the young couples were friendly?"

"Yes, for some time. Mrs. Willet and the child would come down for the summer and Mr. Willet would join them on weekends. They had cocktails with the Highsmiths almost every week."

"What do you mean, 'for some time'?"

He made a slight gesture with one hand, as if pushing something invisible away from him. "The children played together, and when they got a little older, Ed Willet used to take them for rides around that meadow above his barn in that old Mitsubishi of his, teaching them how to drive in a place where they couldn't hurt themselves or anybody or anything else. That sort of thing. The families were friendly. Then something came between them and they grew apart. The Willets suddenly didn't seem to want their daughter playing with the Highsmith children anymore, and that drove a wedge between the parents."

"What was the problem?"

"Like I told you, I'm not an expert on children." He frowned. "I've lost hope of ever understanding why they do what they do."

"You must have some idea."

"I really don't." His hands curled into loose fists.

I studied him, then said, "The night of the beach party the Willet girl went off with the Highsmith children and a boy named Biff Collins. When they found the drowned girl, she was naked. Did the end of the friendship between the Willets and the Highsmiths have to do with sex? Did it happen about the time the children reached puberty?"

His voice was reluctant. "I guess it did."

"Before the estrangement, did the children spend a lot of time together during the summers?"

He hesitated, then nodded. "Yes. When they were little, Heather Willet would come here and play with Gregory and Belinda. There was a path between the houses so she didn't need to get near the road; it was very safe."

I thought of the trail my children had found.

"But that stopped when they got older," I said.

"Yes."

"And you think perhaps her parents were afraid that their daughter was becoming sexually involved with Gregory?"

He drew himself up. "I never said that. I wouldn't know. I suppose it's possible."

"You say that Heather came here to play. Did Gregory and Belinda go to her house sometimes?"

Lines appeared in his forehead. "As they grew older they rarely went to the Willet house. Heather usually came here."

"Why was that?"

"I don't know."

"Can you guess? Were the Willets too strict? Some parents are. Their households are too controlled for children to enjoy themselves. Was that the case?"

"I don't know."

"Later, the Willets didn't want their daughter to visit Gregory and Belinda. Had they disliked the Highsmith children from the first?"

"No. For years, the families got along very well. It was only later when they stopped socializing."

"Then why didn't Gregory and Belinda go visit Heather more often?"

His eyes became emotionless as glass. "Gregory and Belinda usually preferred their own company to that of friends. I think Heather was more interested in them than they were in her."

"Didn't they have other friends? At school, for instance? They were at the beach party with other kids they knew, after all."

"Henry and Abigail enjoyed socializing and the children attended school parties and the like. I don't mean to imply that they were hermits."

"What are you trying to imply?"

"Nothing. Nothing! I'm not implying anything. I'm just upset about everything that's happened."

Again, he touched his forehead with his kerchief. I said, "The night of the beach party, Heather went off with them and a boy named Biff Collins. Were Gregory and Belinda friendly with Collins?"

"I think the boy is Gregory's friend, but I don't really know him well. Don't you think you should be trying to catch a killer instead of asking all these questions about the children? They've just suffered a terrible tragedy. Their father is dead and their mother may be dying."

His face was growing red and I wondered if he was feeling chest pains. I put out my hand and he automatically took it. "Thanks for your help," I said. "If you think of anything else, please call the Chilmark police or the state police."

"I will."

I turned, but stopped at the door. "One more thing. You and your wife have been loyal employees of the Highsmiths for years. My impression is that you're almost part of the family, and that in the normal course of things you would enjoy a few more years of work followed by a comfortable retirement. But if Abigail Highsmith should die, what will happen?"

He gave me a miserable look. "I don't know. I suppose it will depend on the lawyers."

"And the children?"

He stared at me. "They're too young to make decisions about the estate."

"But in five years Gregory will be twenty-one."

His eyes were hooded. He nodded and turned back to the workbench, and I went outside. There was more I wanted to ask, but I didn't like the way he was breathing, and I didn't want to cause another stress attack.

I looked past the house, hoping to see Belinda and Gregory and their uncle coming back, but no one was in sight. To the west, through a gap in the trees, I could see part of a meadow and the cupola of a barn about where I thought the Willet place should be. I guessed that the path Heather Willet had taken in better days probably ran through that gap.

I glanced at the house and thought I saw a window curtain fall back into place. Was Wilma hoping that I'd go or hoping that I wouldn't?

I called to Joshua and Diana and they came around the western corner of the garage.

"Hey, Pa! We found a garden and a trail. This is a good place to explore!"

"Get into the truck and I'll show you where the trail leads."

We got into the Land Cruiser and I drove down to Middle Road, thinking about loyalty. It was a characteristic that most people admired, but one that I had long looked at with a certain skepticism, since Hitler and Attila the Hun had followers as loyal or more loyal than the disciples of the saint of your choice. My stint as a Boston police officer had made it clear that it was a rare criminal who didn't have loyal supporters, and, as many sports critics have maintained, few people are more mindless than loyal sport fans, a typical crowd at a game being a primitive animal with a thousand heads and mouths, but no brain.

That the Shelkrotts were loyal to the Highsmiths was clear, but I wondered whether in this case that was an admirable or a suspect trait. I decided not to decide just yet.

At Middle Road, I turned right and drove to the next set of mailboxes. There I turned right again and approached the Willet house.

18

The Willet house was a large, white-clapboard Cape with a brick chimney rising from the center of its roof. Behind it was the barn whose cupola I'd seen from the Highsmith place. The gravel driveway widened into a turning circle in front of the barn, and large sliding doors suggested that the building was now being used in part as a garage. There were dusty windows in the barn through which I could faintly see what looked like a small school bus. The walkway leading to the front door of the house was lined with early summer flowers, some of which were beginning to droop for lack of water.

The kitchen door of the house, which was closer to the driveway and barn, was clearly the door of choice for the family, as is often the case in New England, where formal front doors are routinely ignored by most people. I guessed that there had been and still might be a mudroom just inside the kitchen door, since the custom of ignoring the front door has its roots in olden times when family and visitors alike had to tramp through mud to get to the house and didn't want to dirty the parlor or living room with their boots. Thus, the kitchen door and the mudroom. Only formal guests would use the front door, and then only on fine days.

I wasn't formal, so I knocked on the kitchen door. There was no answer and I'd expected none. Still, the mowed lawn and generally well-kept look of the place suggested that a caretaker had been at work recently, and I hoped he or she might still be around.

I circumnavigated the house and shouted a few hellos, but no one appeared. I considered using my lock picks, but wasn't nosy enough to actually do it. I'd gotten the picks years before at a yard sale given by a woman who was getting rid of her deceased husband's things and who had no idea at all what the picks were. I hadn't enlightened her, but I had wondered if her husband had been more than the simple carpenter he was known to have been.

Normally I kept my picks at home, but today they were in my pocket and would remain there, for the likelihood seemed dim indeed that I might find some hint in the house about why the Willets had broken relations with the Highsmiths or maybe even had planned a murder and carelessly left the plans behind on the living room table. I didn't mind breaking the law, but I preferred to do it for a good reason, and I didn't have one now.

So I didn't explore the house and returned to my truck, where Joshua and Diana were waiting. But then curiosity got the best of me.

I let the kids out and pointed at the meadow on the hill behind the barn.

"If you go up to that field," I said, "I believe you'll find the trail you saw at the other house. I think the trail runs between the houses. You go explore and tell me if I'm right."

They thought that was a good idea and ran up the hill while I went to the barn. The big doors were padlocked, but by squinting I could see enough through the cobwebbed windows to note that what I had thought was a school bus was in fact an elderly yellow, short-wheel-base Mitsubishi Pajero, an early-bird entry in the now wildly popular SUV market. My guess was that it was the Willets' island car; too beat up for mainland use but just fine for Vineyard beaches and back roads and for teaching your daughter and her friends how to drive in your meadow. I understood that reasoning well, since my father had taught me to drive in a neighbor's field. My opinion of the Willets went up a bit.

I turned and took in their view of the Vineyard hills and green pastures and of the distant sea. It was a fine one, but I could not imagine a worse fate than the death of one's child, and I wondered if Heather's drowning would ever allow the Willets to enjoy this beauty again. The Buddha might still be able to smile, but neither I nor the Willets were the Buddha.

I walked up the hill and agreed with my children that the trail clearly led from the Willet meadow to the Highsmith house but vetoed the idea of continuing on to the Highsmiths'.

We got back into the truck and I drove down-island, full of fuzzy impressions and questions. In Edgartown, I took a left on Pease's Point Way, a right onto Morse, and a left onto Fuller Street, where, amid the street's lovely white houses, I came to Manny Fonseca's woodworking shop. Manny's shop was one of my children's favorite dangerous places and I had worked hard to teach them to stay clear of the saws and other woodworking machines and tools.

Manny Fonseca, the Portagee Pistoleer, lived, breathed, dreamed, bought, sold, and fired guns, pistols in particular. He was a crack shot, a member and loud defender of the NRA, and Zee's pistol instructor. He had, in years past, been an equally loud and public critic of the local Wampanoags who lived up in what was then Gay Head but was now the town of Aquinnah, accusing them of being "professional Indians" since they had made a big effort to be recognized as an official tribe only when there was some money to be made from it. Then, to the amusement of many, including me, Manny had discovered that an ancestral romance legally qualified *him* to be a Wampanoag, and thereafter he had turned his only partially good-humored criticism toward the non-Indian invaders of the nation in general and the island in particular.

Aside from his firearms expertise, Manny was also a first-class finish carpenter who was constantly kept busy by the mansionizers who were energetically buying properties, tearing down whatever buildings were already on the land, and building houses that were bigger and better than any previously known to the island. Manny limited his contracts and charged absurd amounts for his work, in part, I thought, so he would have more time to play with his beloved guns and to coach Zee for her pistol competitions. For Zee, a dedicated opponent of violence, had, with Manny's enthusiastic help, discovered that she was, ironically, a natural with a handgun and that she greatly enjoyed competitive shooting. I had once been a policeman, but Zee could shoot circles around me.

We went into the shop, inhaling the sweet smell of woods and oils, and I repeated my traditional warnings to the kids about dangerous tools and machines.

"We know, Pa. We'll just look."

I kept an eye on them anyway, as they walked and looked, eager to touch but keeping their hands to themselves.

Manny was at a workbench, fitting together the pieces of a custom bureau. He glanced over his shoulder then turned back to his work, clamping one board to another. When the work satisfied him, he again turned to me and smiled.

"Hi, kids. Hello, J.W. What brings you to my humble Native American shop? Do you have some trinkets you'd like to exchange for my property?"

"Sure, if you're willing to trade."

"We've smartened up since 1626. No more Manhattans for twenty-four dollars' worth of knickknacks."

"Too bad. I could resell this place for a lot more than twenty-four bucks. I might even make enough money to live on Nantucket for a week or two."

"I don't know if you'd get that much, but you might manage a midweek two-day rental in the off-season. Your wife is shooting better and better, by the way. She tell you that I told her she should try out for the Olympic team?"

"No. Did you?"

"Yeah. I got myself a Feinwerkbau a while back, so she can practice for the air pistol competition, and I'm getting a Walther O.P. for the rapid fire. I think she can do real good in either one or both if she sets her mind to it. She is a genuine natural. She's already getting better than me."

High praise. "I'll talk with her about it," I said. "It'd be nice to have an Olympic athlete in the family, but it might depend on how much time she has to train. She doesn't like to be away from the hospital too long. Remember how they wanted her to go out to Hollywood? She said thanks but no thanks."

"I remember," he said. "Those folks who made that movie here a few years back wanted her to go west so they could make her famous, but she told them she'd rather be a nurse than a movie star, and besides, she had a family to take care of. What brings you downtown, J.W.? Come summer, you usually hang around up there in the woods until after Labor Day."

I got right to the point. "You used to shoot with the

father of the Willet girl who drowned up at Great Rock. Were you and he friendly or was it just a casual acquaintance?"

He shook his head, then, as people often do, answered a question that hadn't been asked. "Terrible thing, that young girl drowning like that. I haven't seen Ed since just after it happened. Hear that he and Geraldine left the island right afterward. She and the girl were there in the house together, you know, and Ed would come down weekends. I guess they both wanted to get away from the place after the drowning. Don't blame them a bit."

"Neither do I. How'd you happen to know Willet?"

He leaned against the workbench and thought back. "I met Ed at the Rod and Gun Club pistol range several summers ago. He likes to come down and plink with his twenty-two. Shoots an old Colt Woodsman when he's here on weekends. We hit it off pretty good, and I showed him a couple of things he didn't know. I guess I'm sort of what they call a father figure for him, him being that much younger than me. He's from out in Michigan originally. Used to shoot as a kid and just kept it up. Nice guy. Met Geraldine a few times. Nice woman. Their girl was a wild one, I guess, but Ed didn't complain too much about her. More the doting-father type, if you know what I mean."

"Up in Chilmark he lived next door to a family named Highsmith. They were friendly for years and their kids played together. He ever talk about that?"

Manny eyed me. "Highsmith's the one who got shot, isn't he? And his wife too, they say. I hear that you and him scuffled a few days earlier. That true?"

I gave him my version of the encounter and told him about being on the golf course when Highsmith's body was found.

"I didn't know you're a golfer, J.W."

"I'm not. I got talked into playing by Glen Norton. Now there are some people who add my scuffle with Highsmith to me being there when we found the body in that sand trap and think I might have something to do with his death. I'm trying to get clear of that idea."

Manny was instantly indignant. "Hell, J.W., anybody knows you, knows you didn't kill him. What bullshit! Oops! Sorry, kids!"

"That's okay," said little Diana, who was nearby, peering at a lathe. "Cow manure is good fertilizer, Pa says."

"Your pa is right," said Manny, relieved.

Diana drifted away and Manny turned back to me. I lowered my voice. "A while back there was some kind of falling-out between the Willets and the Highsmiths after they'd been friends for years. I think it had to do with their children but I don't know any more than that. Did Ed Willet ever talk about it with you?"

"You don't think Ed Willet shot Highsmith, do you? Hell, Ed and Geraldine weren't even on the island when that happened. Besides, Ed wouldn't ever shoot anybody. I think he's some kind of Quaker, in fact."

"A Quaker who likes to shoot?"

"Why not? He just doesn't like the idea of shooting people. Like Zee, for gosh sakes. She wouldn't hurt a fly."

Zee had, in fact, ended the career of many a fly, tick, and mosquito, and had once shot a couple of thugs in self-defense, but he'd made his point.

"I'd still like to know what happened to sour the relationship between the Willets and the Highsmiths. It seemed to happen when the kids reached puberty."

Manny's face became wary. "You're putting me in a hard spot, J.W. I'm not sure I want to pass on what Ed said. I might have got it wrong in the first place and you might get it wronger because I got it wrong."

Good old Manny. A nice guy even though he did belong to the NRA. I said, "I'm in a hard spot myself, Manny. There are people on this island who think I may have cacked Henry Highsmith. I'd like to prove them wrong."

"But you didn't kill him."

"But they think I might have. You said that Heather Willet was a wild one. What do you mean? It must have been something her father said."

"The girl's dead, J.W. It's not right to speak ill of the dead."

He didn't like this conversation, but I pushed it. "What ill is that, Manny? You can't hurt her now. She's past hurt. If it's that she might have been sexually active at fifteen, you won't be telling me anything I haven't already heard. That night she went off with two boys and another girl, and she was naked when they found her body. Is that it? Is that what made her father call her wild?"

Manny rubbed his jaw and dropped his own voice. "I'm getting to be a stuffy old man. All this modern sex stuff you see on TV seems a little too much to me. Maybe what goes on between grown-ups is okay, but what the kids know and do worries me. I don't like it."

"So it was her sexual activity that bothered her father. Is that why he broke off with the Highsmiths? So Heather wouldn't spend so much time with Gregory Highsmith?"

He seemed to search for words. Then he said, hesitantly and slowly, "Yeah, that was part of it, but there was more, I think. He didn't like what he saw in the Highsmith kids after they got older. He didn't want Heather to hang out with them anymore."

"Why not?"

Manny frowned and flicked his eyes toward Joshua and Diana. "I'm not really sure. Ed didn't say much and he was careful when he talked, but he let things slip out sometimes. I may have heard him wrong or misinterpreted what he said, but one thing I remember is that when he told Henry and Abigail Highsmith that Heather wouldn't be going over to their house anymore, neither of them seemed surprised or argued. He said it was as if they had been expecting it."

"But Heather was at the beach party and so were Gregory and Belinda, and she had gone off with the Highsmiths and a boy named Biff Collins when she drowned. That doesn't sound like a broken friendship between the kids."

Manny looked at me. "I don't think Heather wanted to break off the friendship. I think she wanted Gregory. I'd be willing to bet that she sneaked out of the house to go to that party and get together with him. It was her parents who didn't want her to keep company with the Highsmith kids."

I thought about that. Four kids sneak out and meet at a beach and a few hours later one of them is dead.

I asked Manny if he could think of any connection between what had happened on the beach and the death of Henry Highsmith and the attack on his wife. He couldn't. I thanked him for his time, collected my children, and headed for the door.

"Talk with Zee about that Olympic idea," said Manny, as I left. "I think she can make the team."

"I'll tell her you mentioned it."

"Make sure you do. She's a natural!"

Outside, Diana the Huntress, who was always on the trail of food, had not forgotten our earlier discussion.

"Pa?"

"What?"

"We're hungry. Can we have lunch at The Bite? Can we have fried clams?"

"Why not? Get into the truck."

19

Back in Menemsha, at The Bite, we had the island's best fried clams for lunch and afterward had ice cream for dessert. It was a proper Vineyard summer meal, and it was shared by others who came to the counter in a steady stream.

Above us, the sun hung high in the blue sky that arced from horizon to horizon, and out beyond the parking lot, the small beach was filled with sunbathers. Beyond them Vineyard Sound glittered over to the Elizabeth Islands, on one of which, long ago, a leper colony had existed. Now that island was a school for troubled boys just a short slide from jail, where they got a last, tough chance to learn to fly right. I admired the people who ran the school but had often wondered how its graduates fared once they got back to their old neighborhoods. Jesus had reportedly observed that the poor would always be among us, and I suspected the same was true of criminals.

One of whom was operational on this side of the sound.

On the way back down-island, my son, who had been patient all morning, spoke.

"Pa?"

"What, Joshua?"

"How come you're looking in the mirror so much?"

"Oh, just checking. When you drive, you check in all directions so you don't hit anything and nobody hits you."

"Pa."

"What, Diana?"

"Are we going to work on the bridge today?"

It was a fair question.

"Sure."

So I put crime on a back burner and we spent the rest of the afternoon making great progress on the bridge. Tarzan would have been proud of us.

Zee was too, when she came home from the hospital and she and I were admiring our handiwork over martinis on the balcony.

"Another day or two and we'll be done," I said. "Then the kids can have their choice of trees: the beech or the oak."

"It'll be almost as good as a real jungle. I hope nobody falls out of a tree and breaks something."

It was a universal and eternal fear of all parents who lived near trees, and one to which I was not immune, although I tried to keep my concerns in check since it was my view that kids had to be allowed to take reasonable chances and to suffer a certain amount of hurt when they fell or ignored warnings. It was, I knew, an old-fashioned idea, but one that I liked better than forbidding them activities that included an element of danger.

I considered telling Zee not to worry, but that advice has never, to my knowledge, kept anyone from worrying; just the opposite, in fact. So I contented myself with pointing out details of the day's construction and at bedtime was satisfied that no one had fallen out of the trees that day. Parenting is a day-by-day phenomenon.

The next day was Zee's day off, and I asked her how she'd like to spend it. The answer was: First she'd like to go to the beach, taking along a couple of rods, of course, in case there were any stray bluefish swimming by. Then she wanted to wash her hair. Both the children and I thought those were proper plans, so I loaded the Land Cruiser with beach gear and put rods in their roof racks while Zee packed a cooler with food and drink.

We drove down to Katama, then shifted into four-wheel drive and headed east over Norton Point Beach. On both sides of us the water danced in the sun.

We found a spot on East Beach, about halfway to Wasque, and spread ourselves out. It was a lovely summer day, with a small southwest wind blowing warm air over the sand and sea. While Joshua and Diana tested the water and dug in the sand, Zee and I took turns sunning ourselves on the big bedspread we used as a beach blanket and wandering down the beach, lazily casting for fish that showed no interest in our lures.

When the fish are biting, you have to keep your mind on what you're doing, but when they're ignoring you and you're just casting and reeling in because you like the feel of doing it, you can think of many other things.

I thought about Glen Norton, Gabe Fuller, and Jasper Jernigan.

I believed I knew Glen well enough to exclude him from my list of murder suspects, but I also knew that more than one citizen has been shocked to discover that his mild, helpful, good-natured, churchgoing neighbor is actually a mass murderer with a backyard full of buried bodies. Still, Glen's expression when he'd uncovered Highsmith's hand and his shaky demeanor afterward suggested that his shock was real. Of course it was possible that he'd killed Highsmith but that someone else had buried the body where Glen had found it. The scenario was unlikely, but would account for Glen's reaction. True crime is generally more straightforward than that, however, so for the time being I set Glen to one side of my mental list of suspects.

Jasper Jernigan and Gabe Fuller were other breeds of cat. I considered Jasper.

On the golf course, he had been a pleasant, light-hearted companion, but I'd seen his letters in the paper and they bespoke a temperament capable of deep resentment and towering passion. He identified so closely with golf that he considered an attack on the proposed Pin Oaks course to be an attack on him personally. I knew political, religious, and other ideological zealots who also took any criticism of their beliefs as an assault on them, and whose passions threatened to run high enough to kill. Sports fans were often such people, which is no surprise since "fan" is short for "fanatic." Many a soccer ref has had to run for his life, and more than one hockey dad has been killed by another as their sons played the game.

I wanted to know more about Jasper, but the person who really interested me was Gabe Fuller, the taciturn man who carried a short-barreled rifle in his golf bag.

As I thought back to those three-plus holes that we'd played, it seemed as clear now as it had then that Gabe was doing double duty as Jasper's bodyguard and golfing pal. I remembered those eyes constantly looking here then there, ahead then back, into the woods then out on the fairway, always moving; I remembered how he rarely strayed far from Jasper, how he never drove too far from where Jasper's errant strokes sent his ball.

Wealth and power breed enemies, and Jasper thereby might need a bodyguard, especially taking into consideration his hot-tempered and acid-tongued attacks on the anti-golf crowd. If those letters were typical of his response to other adversaries, I suspected that there might be a lot of people out there who would not weep at the news of Jasper's demise or who, indeed, might be glad to assist in that consummation.

If so, Gabe was just the man for Jasper: a capable bodyguard who was at the same time a pleasant and capable golf partner.

My time with Jasper and Gabe had been brief, but long enough that I'd gotten the impression that Jasper's trust in Gabe was near total; Gabe's loyalty to Jasper, on the other hand, was harder for me to assess, for while Jasper showed his emotions, Gabe's face had revealed little.

Just how loyal was Gabe? Was he one of those soldiers who would step between his employer and a gunman even as the trigger was being pulled? Was he one who would not reason why, but would ride into the valley of death, sabering the gunners and charging an army while all the world wondered?

And would he go farther? Was he one who would, without hesitation or question, assassinate his master's enemies, who wouldn't spare a sigh though worlds of wanwood leafmeal lie?

If so, was Jasper so mad at Henry Highsmith that he'd sent Gabe not only to shoot him but to bury him in what Henry might have equated with a pit of excrement, a final insult even after death?

I reached back in my memory and recalled Jasper following the discovery of Highsmith's body. Glen had been quite distressed, but Jasper had shown much less reaction initially, and had seemed totally collected by the time the police had arrived.

Hmmmm.

Gabe had shown no emotion at all, although he'd assured Glen that he, too, had been rattled. I hadn't believed him then and I didn't believe him now.

Another thought: maybe Gabe had killed Highsmith without being ordered to do so, motivated by what he took to be the unstated wishes of his boss, or by a loyal wish to silence an enemy before he became more dangerous. A preemptive strike, as it were; such strikes were, after all, quite popular these days in very high war-making circles, and Gabe might have felt that what was good for the nation was good for Jasper.

Or maybe Gabe had misunderstood some remark Jasper had made. It wouldn't be the first time a crime had been committed because of a misunderstanding. I thought of an earlier Henry's four loyal knights and of Becket.

I changed my redheaded Roberts for metal, put my back into a cast, and sent my lure far out into the dancing sea. Maybe there was a stray blue chugging along out there and I'd hit him on the nose. Fishermen spend a good amount of time changing lures, usually to no avail. Sometimes, however, the trick works, and instead of reeling in empty lines, you start to catch fish.

Not this time.

I made another half dozen casts in vain, and walked back to the truck.

"No fish, huh, Pa?"

"No fish, Diana." I put the rod on the roof rack and got a Sam Adams out of the cooler. It was still morning on Martha's Vineyard but somewhere the sun was over the yardarm. The beer was cool and good and I once again considered the idea that God is, among other things, a brewer.

I admired Zee as she lay, bikini clad, eyes closed, on the beach blanket, and with my imaginary camera took an imaginary photo of her and stored it away in the mental file that held many other such pictures. Then I finished my beer and took a quick swim as a substitute for a cold shower.

Family-loaded SUVs moved along the beach, and gradually, to the north and south of us, umbrellas went up, blankets and chairs came out, and the water filled with old and young bodies. By noon the beach was lined with worshippers of sun, sand, and water much like ourselves.

Lunch was chicken salad sandwiches, potato chips, and half-sour pickles, with homemade chocolate chip cookies for dessert. Drink was sodas or beer. My children, superior specimens though they might be, had the soft drinks. At home they'd long since had sips of beer and wine upon request, but neither fancied alcohol when sodas were available.

Afterward I lay beside Zee, pleasantly full-bellied and feeling lazy. I took her hand and held it, listening to our children's voices as they played nearby and feeling Highsmith's tragedy slip away as I slid into a semi-sleep.

But then, in that sleep, I half dreamed of Highsmith's killer and wondered if Neptune's great oceans had washed clean his hands or if those hands had turned the oceans red; if he smiled or groaned during his days; if his murder had murdered his sleep.

I woke up feeling discontent, with sweat covering my body. I had another swim and felt better, and started thinking about the Willets.

In spite of Manny Fonseca's confidence that Ed Willet couldn't be a killer, if the reports I'd gotten were true, both Ed and his wife were logical suspects in the shootings of the Highsmiths. They had broken off relations with the Highsmiths, and had forbidden Heather to have any more to do with the Highsmith children. Heather Willet's drowning had occurred when she had gone off with Gregory and Belinda Highsmith; someone had run Abigail Highsmith off the road shortly after the drowning, and soon after that both Henry and Abigail Highsmith had been shot; Ed Willet owned and practiced with a .22 pistol, the caliber of gun that had been used to shoot both Henry Highsmith and his wife.

The motive would be revenge, with one or both of the Willets blaming the Highsmiths for their daughter's death in the forbidden company of the Highsmith children. The irrationality of that idea didn't make it less possible, because murder is often an irrational act triggered by next to nothing: a spilled drink, the last piece of pie, an imagined slight. Cain killed Abel; Smerdyakov committed patricide; Abraham would have killed Isaac as a religious duty. It doesn't take much to provoke a killing.

Zee's voice recalled me to the present.

"It's almost two. I think we've had enough sun for the day, and if we leave now there shouldn't be much of a line at the ferry."

Her words made me conscious of my heated skin and that the temptation of paradise is to linger in it too long.

We sent the kids into the water for a last swim as we packed up, then wrapped them in their big towels as we drove home. We returned by the Chappy ferry, where, sure enough, the waiting line was short since most people were still at the beach.

Two of the little three-car On Time ferries were crisscrossing between Chappy Point and Edgartown, and sail- and powerboats were going in and out of the harbor through the channel. To our right the beach at the foot of the Edgartown lighthouse was alive with sunbathers, and far out on distant Cape Pogue, the tiny white lighthouse could barely be seen. It was a scene distantly removed from murder.

At home, I chose to be last in the outdoor shower. While the others washed off their salty skins and Zee washed her long black hair, I made a call to Dom Agganis and asked if I could come by in a half hour or so.

Dom said yes, and that Olive had some news for me.

20

Dom was putting papers in a file cabinet when I entered his office.

"I'd like to get my hands on the guys who said computers were going to do away with paperwork," he growled.

"You'll get no sympathy from me," I said. "My kids and wife use our computer more than I do, and my only paperwork is paying bills once a month."

"I can't interest you in a job as my secretary, eh? Not that the state would ever spring for a secretary."

"If they did, do you think I'm cute enough to qualify?"

"Absolutely not. You been out in the sun, or have you been drinking more than usual?"

I touched my hot red nose. "My noon nap on the beach is responsible. If I get skin cancer I plan to sue the guys who made the beer that put me to sleep."

"You can't sneeze without getting sued these days," said Dom. "You want to hear a lawyer joke? No? I don't blame you. How about a blond lawyer joke? What's the definition of gross ignorance?"

"I'm afraid to guess."

"One hundred forty-four blond lawyers." Dom sat down behind his desk. "What brings you here? I think this is the first time you ever called first, so it must be something you want me to tell you about the Highsmith business. Before you ask, the answer is no comment."

"Don't be so hasty. I'm not looking for secrets. Besides, I may have some information to trade. First, though, how's Abigail Highsmith doing?"

"A little better."

"Anybody talk with her yet?"

"Not that much better. What's this information you think I might want?"

I told him of my conversations with the Shelkrotts and my speculations about the Willets. As I did, Olive Otero wandered in from somewhere out back.

Dom leaned back and cupped his head in his big hands. "We've already interviewed the Shelkrotts and we got the same stories except for the part about the girl going to a Swiss school. And your bright idea that the Willets should be on the usual list of suspects is old hat to us. Too bad for your info-trading scheme, but what you have is worth zilch."

"What do you make of the split between the Willets and the Highsmiths?"

He shrugged. "I'm not a shrink or a sociologist. Spats happen for no reason at all sometimes."

"But sometimes there's a good reason. Do you know what it was this time?"

He hesitated, then said, "Not yet. We plan to ask the Willets when we see them."

The hesitation interested me. "Do you know where the Willets were when the Highsmiths got shot?"

"It's none of your business, but they were out in Michigan, where he came from originally. Getting away from home for a while, I guess."

I could understand the desire to get far from the scene of a tragedy, to some place where grief could burn itself out.

"Are they still out there?"

"I haven't heard that they're back in New Haven."

I asked him what he thought of the vengeful-professor theory.

His smile was sarcastic. "It's pretty rare for some pointy-headed professor to blow a colleague away. They're all talk and no action."

"I think we used to call that sort of comment a sweeping generalization. How about the Webster-Parkman case?"

"Exception to the rule. Besides, that happened a hundred and fifty years ago when the West was still wild and young men were going there anyway. No wusses in those days, not even at Harvard. Not like now."

"What about John Skye?" I said. "You know him. He punched cows in Colorado when he was a kid and he still goes out that way every year or so to camp and chase brook trout. He's no wuss."

Dom feigned a yawn. "Another exception to the rule."

"Your rule has a lot of exceptions."

Dom brought his hands down and leaned on his elbows. "If you're trying to find out if we're getting cooperation from the police in Connecticut, I'll save you some time and tell you that we are. There's no evidence that anybody at Yale wanted to off Henry Highsmith. All the tempests there were the teapot kind. And the same goes for Brown. The Rhode Island police have been to Brown and haven't found a single rumor about anyone who might have wanted to murder Abigail Highsmith or her husband. Is that what you came here to find out? If so, you got a lot out of me and I got next to nothing out of you, so you should be happy."

I touched my nose again. Still hot. When I got home I'd smear it with green slime. "I'd be really happy if I knew that your ace investigators actually are ace investigators and got everything right when they nosed around."

"It's an imperfect world, J.W. Maybe they missed the confession written in blood on the college president's door, but I doubt it. Besides, until we find the shootist, the case will stay open and our people will keep asking questions. If there's somebody out there in university-land who packs the right twenty-two under his academic gown, we'll get him eventually. Hell, he'll probably confess. A lot of those sensitive, intellectual types think they're Raskolnikov and want you to know it."

I leaned over and peered at his mouth. "You know, I think that with a little more rehearsal you could be a contender in the International Curled Lip Championships."

He laughed. "You think I need more practice, eh?"

"Not a lot, but some."

"I've got some news for you," said Olive. "One of the guys in that car that followed you couldn't keep the story to himself in the Fireside last night. I found him this morning and persuaded him that it won't be in his best interest if he and his pals try it again. You won't be surprised to learn that they're some of the hotter heads in the cycle crowd."

"Why, thank you, Officer Otero," I said. "I'm in your debt. I don't suppose you'd care to give me the young man's name."

"No, I don't suppose I would, but I don't think you'll have any more trouble with him or his pals. If you do, let me know."

"Olive thinks I should watch *Tarzan and the Leopard Woman*," said Dom. "She's been in a cheerful mood ever since you mentioned it. Maybe you've finally won her heart, J.W."

"Ye gods," said Olive.

"Since you're in a talkative mood," I said to Dom, "what can you tell me about Gabe Fuller?"

"Why should I tell you something about Gabe Fuller?"

"Because he's close to Jasper Jernigan and there was no love lost between Jasper and Henry Highsmith and because Gabe Fuller was carrying some sort of long gun in his golf bag the last time I saw him."

Agganis's eyes narrowed. "Was he now."

"I take him to be Jasper's bodyguard. Don't tell me you missed the gun."

Agganis looked more than annoyed. "I didn't look in his golf bag and he didn't mention any gun when we interviewed him. Come to think of it, when we asked him about his job, he just said he was Jernigan's assistant, and Jernigan never said anything different. I guess I'll be having another talk with those gentlemen."

"There's no law against having a bodyguard or being one."

"Yeah? Well, this is a murder case, and I don't like people holding out on me! Especially people with guns!"

Had I ever seen him so openly irked before? I fed the flame by giving him my thoughts about Gabe as the possible murderer.

"I don't know enough about Mr. Fuller to go that far," said Dom, "but I damn well plan to find out all there is to know. Now, unless you have some other tales to tell me, thanks and good-bye."

"One other thing. Just when was Highsmith killed? He hadn't been in that sand very long, from the looks of him."

"It'll probably be in the papers anyway, so I guess I can tell you. He was plugged the evening before you found him, according to the ME. His wife claims that he was out on his daily bike tour and never came home."

"If he was on his bike tour, where's his bike?"

"You're smart. You tell me."

He was reaching for his telephone when I went out the door.

At home, Zee was making black beans and rice for supper. It was an excellent, simple meal. I inhaled appreciatively.

"Your nose is red," she said, accepting a kiss. "You'd better put some green slime on it."

I went into the bathroom and did that and my nose immediately felt better.

The kids were still outside, playing in the long summer dusk. I went back to the kitchen and poured two vodkas on the rocks. I handed one to Zee and leaned on a counter.

"Cheers," said Zee, lifting her glass. "What did you learn from Dom?"

"That the Willets were in Michigan when the Highsmiths were shot, that there are no professorial suspects at the moment, and that Dom didn't know Gabe Fuller kept a gun in his golf bag."

"And what did he learn from you?"

"That Gabe had a gun in his golf bag and that I think he's Jasper Jernigan's bodyguard and a possible murder suspect." I gave her my Gabe-as-murderer scenarios.

She stirred the rice and beans. "If Dom didn't know that Gabe had a gun, he probably couldn't tell you much else about him either."

"I'd like to know more than I do."

"And Jasper Jernigan's a mystery too."

"I'd like to know where he was when Highsmith was killed."

"I imagine that Dom already has that information."

"I wonder who gave it to him."

She dipped her wooden spoon into the skillet and lifted it first to her own lips, then to mine. "What do you think?"

"Delish. Do you want wine or beer to go with it?"

"Red wine."

"Call the kids and tell them that we're ready to eat."

I went out and did that, and they swung down from the tree house on the rope hung for that purpose, then went right to the outdoor shower, where, in its own alcove, we had an outdoor washbasin too, for hands too dirty to bring into the house.

I poured the house red for the big people and water for the kids and we had a fine meal to end the day. Afterward I washed the dishes and stacked them in the drier, since it's a Jackson rule that whoever doesn't cook does the dishes. I got back to the living room in time to see the end of a hand of five-card stud, won by Joshua, with Zee coming in second. She watched him sweep in the chips. His pile of chips showed that he was doing very well.

"It's about time for bed," said Zee.

"Aw! Just one more hand."

"All right, one more hand. Ante up, everybody. Deal, Diana."

"Ma?"

"What?"

"It's summer, so can we read in bed instead of having to go to sleep right away?"

"Yes, you can. You can read all night if you want to." The children exchanged pleased looks. "Really?"

"Really," Zee said as she dealt. "You're on vacation. Your bet, Diana."

Diana, showing a six of clubs, reluctantly bet. Joshua,

on a roll, raised. Zee saw the bet and Diana wisely folded.

When the last card was dealt. Zee's king-jack was still high but she passed. Joshua bet the limit and his eyes widened when his mother saw his bet and raised.

Was it a bluff?

Joshua peeked at his hole card, frowned, and raised ten more. Zee raised him back. He looked at her and called.

Her two kings beat his two queens and she pulled in the big pot.

"It's called sandbagging," I said to Joshua. "You pretend you don't dare bet, then after everybody else feels confident and bets high, you raise so you can win a big pot."

"Is that fair?" asked irked Joshua.

"There's no rule against it."

"It doesn't seem fair to me."

"You can do it too," I said. "Just make sure you have a good hand when you do."

"Ma, how did you know you had a better hand?"

"I'm your mother. Mothers always know."

"It was mean, Ma."

"It wasn't mean, it was poker," said Zee.

"Bedtime," I said.

"Pa?"

"What, Joshua?"

"Will you teach us how to play Texas Hold'em?"

"Sure, but not right now."

It was a beautiful night, so when the cards and chips were stored away and the kids were in bed, Zee and I sat on our balcony and looked up at the stars.

"You don't think I was mean, do you?" asked Zee.

"Maybe a little bit, but it was a cheap lesson. You took his chips but it didn't cost him any real money. My poker schooling was more expensive."

"I think I'll make a pie tomorrow."

I put my arm around her shoulders. "That should heal his wounds and make you feel better."

It seemed like a good time to tell her about Olive's good news, but as I opened my mouth the phone began to ring. It kept on ringing until I got downstairs and answered it.

"Mr. Jackson?"

It was a voice I didn't know. "Yes."

"Is this the same Mr. Jackson who talked to the Shelkrotts yesterday?"

"Yes."

"My name is Gregory Highsmith. You asked questions about me and my sister. Why don't you come back tomorrow so we can talk. I can tell you whatever you'd like to know. Can you be here about ten o'clock?"

"Yes."

"I look forward to seeing you."

The phone clicked in my ear. I hadn't contributed much to the conversation.

21

I arrived at the Highsmith house exactly at ten, sans children this time since Zee was off work for a second day. The Volvo was parked in front of the garage, but the Chevy station wagon I'd seen before was gone.

Before I could reach the house, the front door opened and three people came out. The eldest was a man about my age who looked rather harried. The other two were much younger and were astonishingly beautiful in both face and form—angelic, almost, like models for Botticelli. I recognized Belinda and Gregory from their pictures and I guessed that the man was their uncle, Tom Brundy.

Belinda Highsmith was slender and ethereal and could have been taken for a woman in her midtwenties as easily as the girl of thirteen I knew her to be. Her hair was long, her foot was light, and her eyes were, at once, wild, innocent, and knowing, curious and bored. I thought of Aeysha and the empire of imagination, and felt drawn and distrustful toward her, as toward some beautiful, feral animal I'd never seen before.

Her brother, only sixteen years old, was a stalwart six-footer, with a high forehead topped with Grecian curls. He had broad shoulders and the walk of a dancer. His facial bones were fine and his skin was clear as a girl's. Like his sister, he was lightly tanned. His feet were small and his hands were large and strong. I had the impression that, if he stripped, his body would mirror Michelangelo's *David*. His eyes, like Belinda's, were pale blue and seemed to shine from within.

They smiled at me in unison and their perfect white teeth gleamed in the morning sun.

But I was looking into those bright blue eyes and seeing secretive teenage creatures peering back at me.

"You're J. W. Jackson," said the man. "I'm Tom Brundy. I understand that you were up here day before yesterday asking some questions. Maybe I can be of help."

Before I could reply, the boy stepped forward and, unlike his uncle, put out his hand. I took it and felt controlled strength.

"I'm Gregory," he said in a friendly baritone. "This is my sister, Belinda. You asked the Shelkrotts about us." He held his smile as he added, "Are you from the police, Mr. Jackson?"

I thought he knew the answer to his question before he asked it.

"Retired," I said, matching his smile with my own.

"Oh," he said. "Wilma and Nathan had the impression that you were an officer of the law, working on the case of the assaults on my parents."

I held my smile. "They were wrong about my being a police officer but right about my working on your parents' case."

"You have no authority to be asking questions," interrupted Brundy. "This family is grieving! Leave us alone! It's illegal for you to impersonate a police officer."

"I just told you that I'm not a police officer," I said to him. "As for authority, mine is that I was there when your brother-in-law's body was found and I'd like to find out how he ended up in that sand trap. As family members you may know who might have hated him and his wife enough to have killed him and attempted to kill her."

"The children and I have discussed that for hours. We can't help you." There was despair in his face and voice.

I looked at the children and saw that Belinda had hooked her arm in Gregory's.

"We don't know anything that might help you," she said in a misty voice. "Uncle Tom is right. We've talked about it and talked about it and none of us know anything." She looked up at her brother. "It's a mystery."

"Yes, it's a mystery," he said. "We just can't imagine who could do such a thing."

"You can tell me one thing," I said. "What happened between your parents and the Willets?" I poked a thumb at the Willets' cupola. "For years they were friends and you and Heather played together. Then, suddenly, the friendship ended. What happened?"

The young people looked at each other, but the uncle was angry. "What difference does it make? That happened years ago!"

"It makes a difference because it might give the Willets a motive for murder."

"That's absurd!"

"And it didn't happen that long ago," I said. "A couple of years, maybe less. Isn't that right, Gregory?"

Gregory held his sister's eyes for a moment longer, then turned to me and nodded. "That's right, Mr. Jackson, and I can tell you why, if . . ."

"You don't have to tell him anything!" cried Brundy.

"I don't mind," said Gregory. "I'm sure the Willets are innocent, but I could be wrong. I don't know why murders happen, but maybe it doesn't take much. Maybe all it takes is a sudden impulse. Is that right, Mr. Jackson? You were a policeman once. Is a sudden impulse all it takes?"

"Sometimes. Tell me why your parents and the Willets ended their friendship."

"It was because of Heather," said Belinda, raising her chin the slightest bit and holding tighter to her brother's arm. "She changed. She began to chase Gregory. She was quite open about it. It got so he couldn't be alone with her. She was shameless. When my parents found out about it, they told the Willets they didn't want Heather coming here anymore. That was when our families ended their friendship."

"Is that what happened?" I asked Gregory. "Did you see it the same way?"

He nodded. "She was a very sensual girl. It got to the point that I was actually afraid of her." He frowned a frown like some I'd seen on film. "You might not believe that someone my size could be frightened by someone her size, but I was. She could fall into an absolute rage when she saw me just talking to some other girl. I was afraid to turn my back to her. It was terrible and it kept getting worse. I didn't know what to do."

Belinda nodded, and looked up at her brother's face. "We were both afraid of her," said her half-whispering voice. "We didn't know what to tell our parents."

"Then, who told them about her? How did they find out?"

"The Shelkrotts. They found out and they told Mom and Dad." The children exchanged looks and nods.

"How did they find out?"

"One day they saw, they heard. Heather was too loud and too close to the house. Usually she waited till she and my brother were alone, till no one was around, but that day she couldn't stop herself, and they found out."

"And that was the end of it? Heather never came here again? You never went to her house again?"

"Never." Gregory and Belinda shook their heads in unison.

"Now you know about the dirty linen," said Tom Brundy. "That was why the friendship ended with the

Willets. They probably didn't believe what they were told about their daughter, and blamed Henry and Abigail for telling lies about her."

"But it wasn't the end of the relationship between you and Heather," I said to the teenagers. "She met you again on the beach that night and went off with you and Biff Collins."

Belinda's eyes widened slightly. "We didn't invite her to the party, but we don't own the beach. She wouldn't stay away when we went with Biff."

"What happened when the four of you were alone?"

"Nothing," said Gregory.

"Tell them the truth," said Belinda, looking up at him before she brought her eyes back to me. "She wanted sex and he wouldn't do it. She stripped off her bathing suit and she tried to put her arms around Gregory, but he pushed her away. She ran down the beach toward the rocks and we never saw her again."

"Where was Biff Collins?"

Belinda seemed to cling harder to Gregory. "Biff is a member of the swimming team at Tuttle School. He'd gone swimming while the rest of us were still walking down the beach. He was way out in the water somewhere. Every now and then he'd shout and tell us to come in, but we never did."

"So he never saw Heather play seductress?"

"I don't think so." Her voice sounded as ethereal as a misty wind. "When he finally swam back, we realized that Heather had been gone a long time and we began to call for her and try to find her. But we never could, so we went back to the others and somebody had a cell phone and called 911 and then we all looked some more until the police came." She stopped speaking, then added breathlessly, "We were afraid she might have committed suicide."

"Aren't you satisfied?" asked Tom Brundy, putting his angry face nearer to mine. "Do you want all the graphic details? The girl was sick, and my niece and nephew have just lost their father!"

I wished I had the Willetts' understanding of their daughter and their version of the friendship between them and the Highsmiths, but I wasn't likely to get that. I wondered if any parents really knew their children. I wondered if I knew mine.

"Is there anything else we can tell you, Mr. Jackson?" Gregory seemed eager. "My sister and I want to help in any way we can."

I looked around and said, "Where are the Shelkrotts? I'd like to talk with them again, but I see that their car is gone."

The three of them exchanged looks. "We don't know," said Tom Brundy. "Yesterday, when I was at the store for groceries, they suddenly left. They didn't say where they were going or why."

"Gregory and I were here with them," said Belinda, "and they just announced that they were leaving. And they did. They didn't even take all of their things. They seemed to be in a hurry, and they said that they wouldn't be coming back."

Possibilities raced through my mind. I said, "Don't you think that's odd?"

Gregory nodded. "Very odd. We wondered if . . . Well, we wondered if they might be trying to escape."

"Escape from what?"

He looked down at Belinda then back up at me. "From the police. We've wondered if maybe they're the ones who killed our father and they're trying to get away, or if maybe they'd just been freaked by everything that's happened."

"Have you called the police?"

"We don't have any proof of anything," said Brundy. "We can't even send in a missing persons report because they left voluntarily."

Gregory nodded. "We can't imagine that they killed our dad. If they did, of course we want them caught."

His sister's shoulder leaned against his arm. "Yes," she said softly and sadly. "We want to help find the evil people who shot poor Mom and Dad."

"We certainly do," said Gregory, putting his hand on his sister's arm. "Is there anything else we can tell you that might help?"

"No, but you should tell the police about the Shelkrotts. If I think of anything more, I'll give you a call."

"Please do," Belinda said.

But their uncle was less willing to see me again. "You've intruded on us quite enough. I want you to stay away and leave these poor mourning children alone!"

"I'm pretty set on finding out who killed their father," I said to him. "I know more now than when I came. It's not enough but it may lead somewhere. If I learn something significant, I'll take it to the police."

I went to my old Toyota. Behind the wheel I gave a last glance toward the house.

Brundy was frowning, Gregory's perfect face was bland, and Belinda's face reminded me of Leonardo's drawing of Saint Anne. I drove away, filled with odd feelings and impressions.

It is said that every crime involves two stories: that of the victim and that of the killer, and that if you know enough about one story, you can discover the other. Since it's common for victims to be murdered by people they know, the two stories are often interwoven before the climactic scene when they come together for the last time and the crime occurs. If there is a detective, then there's also a third story. When his or her story meets that of the killer in a final scene, justice may be done.

I was already scanning the stories of possible killers, including the Willets, the Shelkrotts, Gabe Fuller, and Jasper Jernigan, but I still knew too little about the Highsmiths' story. I wanted to know it better, because somewhere along the line, their story and that of the killer or killers may have crossed.

I thought about what I'd just seen and heard and tried to sort out my impressions of the young Highsmiths and their uncle. Brundy, like the Shelkrotts, the only adults I'd met at the house, was totally different from the children. All three adults were angry and secretive, whereas the brother and sister seemed to share a powerful strength that shielded them from the shock of their parents' fates and let them be open and calm.

Or were they as open and free from shock as they appeared? Like many teenagers, they had something of a theatrical air, as though they were playing parts they knew well and acted out when in the presence of adults. It was a very human thing to do: play a particular role for a particular audience. Who among us shows the same face to the cop who gives him a ticket as he shows later when telling the tale to friends? Who plays the same part at work as he plays in a sweetheart's bed?

And what of Brundy and the Shelkrotts? They too had doubtless been wearing masks when they talked to me. And what of me? I had worn a few different masks myself during the past few days.

Where were the Shelkrotts, and why had they suddenly gone away?

It was not yet noon, but I felt like I'd put in a full day. I drove to Oak Bluffs, actually found a parking place on Circuit Avenue, and went to the Fireside for a burger and a Sam Adams.

The Fireside is a bit on the grungy side. It smells of illegal cigarettes and even more illegal grass, but its beer is good and it serves excellent pub grub, so it draws a good crowd from the college and young working set. I got there just before the noon rush and was finishing my lunch while the main crowd was still filing in. I wondered if any of the guys in the car to whom Olive had spoken were among today's customers. If so, they avoided giving me any angry glances.

My friend Bonzo, who sweeps and cleans and otherwise makes himself handy at the Fireside, wasn't in sight, so he couldn't ID the cycle and golfing hotheads who had duked it out the previous weekend, if any were there, and I didn't get any of the latest OB gossip. Bonzo is short on heavy thinking, thanks to a youthful experience with bad acid, but he has big ears and sharp eyes to go along with his heart of gold, and he often knows what's going on or at least what customers think is going on. I was hoping to get the latest rumors about the Highsmith shootings, but such was not to be, so I paid up and drove to John Skye's farm.

22

John Skye's place was off the Edgartown–West Tisbury road. He and his wife, Mattie, and their twin daughters summered there when they weren't summering in southwest Colorado, on his old family ranch near Durango. I closed down their island farm in the fall, looked after it during the winter, and opened it up again in the spring, making whatever minor repairs were needed, turning on the water, raking the lawns, airing the place out, and laying in basic supplies. Over the years, Zee and I had gotten quite close to John and Mattie.

John taught at Weststock College, north of Boston, during the winter. His current literary project was the writing of a definitive book on swordsmanship and fencing, a subject that had taken his fancy far back in his undergraduate days when he'd been a three-weapon man. His battered collegiate saber, foil, and épée were now triangulated behind his rusty mask on a wall of his library, my favorite room in his old farmhouse.

As I drove into John's yard I could see the twins, Jill and Jen, riding past the barn and corrals, headed for the bridle path in the woods beyond their far fence. They were now college women, but had been horse lovers since childhood. There has been a lot written about the love of girls for horses, but the love is a lot more certain than the arguments explaining it. Equine power, beauty, size, and speed, combined with female sexuality, are elements in most of the theories, and I was not about to argue. What I knew for certain was that an amazing percentage of women and girls loved horses. My own Diana was already showing signs of such affection, in fact. If there was a *Tarzan and the Horse Woman* movie, she'd probably want to watch it every day.

The twins recognized the old Land Cruiser and waved but didn't stop. Why should they? They could see me anytime.

I parked in front of the house and checked things out. All seemed well and as I walked to the door, Mattie came around the corner of the house, pulling off gardening gloves. She smiled, glanced at the truck, and gave me a kiss.

"Where's Zee?"

"At home with the kids. Is John in? I'd like to talk with him."

"I keep telling him that on a day like this he should be outside getting some exercise, but instead he's in the library staring at his computer, doing research for that book of his." She became conspiratorial. "Do me a favor and take him for a walk while you talk. Can you do that?"

"I can try."

John, in fact, was ready for a walk. "You could spend forever on the damned Internet! Ruin your eyes! I can use a break. Let me get my stick."

He found a floppy hat and the crooked walking stick he favored when he strolled the island's many trails, and we set out, walking in the direction his daughters had taken earlier.

"They used to call a walk like this a constitutional," he said. "Maybe they still do. Good for what ails you, whatever it's called."

"How's the book coming?"

"The research is fun. I'm still trying to outline the book itself. People have been using swords for war and sport for a long time, so there's a lot of information and I need to organize it in a way that makes it easy to get at. I hate these damned tomes that have information that you can't find without a research assistant."

"I thought the first requirement of scholarship was the love of drudgery."

He threw me a smile. "Well, there's something to that. Digging around in dusty old boxes and books has a certain appeal. But I don't see any point in writing a definitive work that's hard to read if I can write one that's easy."

"So it's still going to be the definitive work, eh?"

"Absolutely."

John had actually already written one definitive work: a new annotated translation of *Gawain and the Green Knight*. It hadn't earned him much money, but it had been well received in the learned journals. What he really wanted, he said, was for people to read the wonderful poem, but it was looking increasingly doubtful that even his fine translation was going to lead thousands of new readers into the delights of Arthurian romance.

So things go in the academic writing game.

We passed through the gate that divided his land from the bridle path that led through the forest beyond. Above us, thin white clouds were floating east across a pale blue sky and at our feet were the tracks of the twins' horses.

"Fine day," said John. "What brings you here when you could just as easily be fishing? Come to think of it, why am I here when I could just as easily be fishing?"

"Mattie might suggest that you could as easily be doing a little weeding in the garden."

"She's probably right, but one of the advantages of being an official intellectual is that we get credit for just thinking about things; we don't actually have to do them. I've offered that argument to Mattie a number of times over the years when she points out that there's work to be done."

"And how does she take it?"

"Not well at all, I must admit. But you're not here to discuss escaping from chores."

"No. A while back you said something about Henry Highsmith being married to a Hatter, and that the Hatters were famous for being wacky. I'd like to hear more about that."

"Are you involved in that case? I thought you promised Zee to stay out of trouble."

"I'm not in trouble."

"I know you had that little wrestling match with Henry just days before he was killed, and that you were one of the people who found the body. And now you're nosing around trying to find out who killed him. If you're not in trouble, it sounds like you're trying to be."

"Some people think I did him in. I didn't, but I'd like to prove it."

"Do you really care what people think?"

"Not as much as some people, but I think that 'decent respect for the opinions of mankind' idea is a pretty good one. Besides, I have a wife and kids who might catch grief because of what people think about me. If I was a hermit, things might be different."

He grunted assent. "Donne was right about none of us being islands. So you want to know something about the Highsmiths that might point you to whoever killed him and shot her, eh? Why don't you tell me what you know, so I don't cover the same ground all over again."

So I did that, telling him again what had happened

in the fish market and then what had happened on the golf course, and what I'd done since: where I'd gone and whom I'd seen and what I'd heard and read. As I spoke, I tried to listen to what I was saying as if the words were coming from someone I didn't know and concerned a subject about which I knew little or nothing. I tried to detect false notes, errant reasoning, confusions between facts and guesswork, between truth and desire, between conviction and suspicion.

John kept silent and when I was done he said, "You told me that you went online and looked up the Highsmiths. My impression is that you paid more attention to Henry than to Abigail. Is that right?"

I thought back. "Yes. I was looking for anything that might suggest that he was a controversial character who could have enemies. Academic ones, maybe, or some ongoing feud with some person or group. But I didn't find anything. When I looked at Abigail's entry, I didn't see anything there, either. But you say she was a Hatter. What are you getting at?"

He waved his crooked walking stick. "The Highsmiths are both well known in the academic world. Henry wasn't the first of his people to go to Harvard, but his grandfather and father were businessmen, not scholars. Henry was the first of his family to make his name in university circles. Henry has—had—the reputation of being a brilliant guy who lived a very conservative and traditional private life, who taught tough, very traditional classes, but who supported liberal causes."

"Like opposing another golf course on the Vineyard, and advocating bicycles instead of SUVs."

"Like that. A personal and professional conservative but a public liberal. His critics might have said he should make up his mind, but he didn't need to. His father and grandfather were the same way. It was in the blood. In any case, there was nothing that I know about Henry Highsmith that made him a logical target for murder." John batted a small rock off the bridle path, using his stick as a golf club.

"I figure that a golf zealot might have done it."

He nodded. "Zealot is the key word there. Fanatics don't need logical reasons to do what they do. Maybe a golf fanatic did shoot him then bury him in the place he'd have most hated being buried. It's crazy, but it's possible. Did you ever meet Abigail Highsmith?"

"No."

"I've seen her at a convention or two. An astonishingly beautiful woman. One of those people who seems to walk on air, with her feet not quite touching the ground. A woman you might be afraid to touch for fear that she was made of mist and your hand would go right through." He glanced at me. "She looks like a faery's child."

I said nothing, but found myself again seeing Belinda Highsmith, holding tight to her brother's arm and gazing at me with those haunting eyes and that Saint Anne smile.

"Of course," said John, "Abigail is actually anything but ethereal. She's a very strong, very physically fit woman, very bright, very ambitious, very driven. She's personable and can be charming, but she runs a tight ship."

"As her husband did."

"Maybe that was one of the attractions between them. But as alike as she and Henry were, they were different in one respect. Do you know anything about the Mad Hatters?"

"I know about the one in Alice, and I've read that real hatters used to go mad because of the mercury in the solutions they used to make felt hats."

"This is a different family of Hatters. There's some speculation that maybe some early members of the family actually were in the hat business, but the generations that I know about were all in the literary-academic-scholarship professions. University professors, publishers, deep thinkers, and the like."

A little door opened in my memory. "I remember now reading that Abigail Highsmith was Abigail Hatter when she met Henry at Harvard."

"Right you are. Abigail was indeed a Hatter, and she was far from the first in her family to attend The World's Greatest University. Her ancestors had been at Harvard and Radcliffe for generations. They were famous for their brilliance but . . ." He swung at another pebble and bounced it only a few feeble feet. He advanced upon it and swung again, this time driving it into the trees. "Bogie. Drat. Where was I? Oh, yes . . . They were brilliant but they were also mad as March hares. Not all of them, of course, but so many that they became known as the Mad Hatters. If you hired a Hatter, you couldn't be sure whether you were getting a genius or a potential opium addict or duelist or babbling idiot. Hatters could be violent or the fanatic protectors of ticks and toads. Some of them were accused of having sexual relations with their dogs and horses, others attacked their dearest friends with sticks and swords and pistols; some of them went to jail, others went into mental hospitals and never came out.

"Of course, most of them weren't strange in any way but were famous lecturers or produced wonderful publications. Sometimes a whole generation would pass without producing a single Mad Hatter. But then, just when you were beginning to relax, Professor Hatter would run naked across the college green waving a cavalry saber and chasing the dean, or would be found crouched under a rosebush babbling that the Martians had come to take him away." John looked at me. "There are several Hatters, most of them apparently very sane, at work as we speak at respectable jobs at major universities and publishing houses and elsewhere. Abigail Highsmith is one of them."

"Do you think the Hatters' madness has something to do with the shootings?"

"I have no idea," said John. "But I think it's something you should consider. You've been spending most of your time trying to discover a logical suspect in the case, someone who had a strong reason to kill the Highsmiths. You've also given thought to the possibility that a fanatic of some kind might be responsible, a fanatic golfer, for instance. Well, even a fanatic usually has a reason for his behavior, no matter how bizarre that reason might seem to someone else; but if your killer is a madman, he doesn't need a reason. All he needs is an impulse." He glanced at me. "The lawyers call it temporary insanity and they can usually find a psychologist who'll testify to it under oath."

"Whoever is behind these shootings had a purpose," I said, "and he remembered it long enough to shoot two people a few days apart. It wasn't a momentary impulse."

John shrugged. "Even madmen sometimes have their reasons." He gestured ahead with his stick. "Beware the fresh horse manure, J.W., or you'll be cleaning your sandals before you get back to solving this crime."

23

When John and I finished our walk, we sat on his patio with Mattie, who had laid aside her gardening gloves and joined us for beer. It's hard to beat a cool beer on a warm day.

"We're abandoning you menfolk tomorrow, you know," she reminded us. "We ladies are taking our four children to New Bedford for the day, to experience American civilization closer at hand."

"By which you mean shopping," said John. "Poor Joshua, going to the city with four women and a girl. I pity him."

"He might like shopping," said Mattie. "Some males do, you know, even if you two characters hate it."

"We manly men don't mind shopping in liquor stores and hardware stores," I said.

"And bookstores," said John. "It's just girly stores that bore us."

"Piff," said Mattie.

"It's not the shopping so much," I said, "it's the differences in the way women shop. When men shop they know what they want and they go and try to find it and then they come home. Women can spend all day just wandering around looking to see what's there. Zee says it's because men are hunters and women are gatherers. Cavemen went hunting a deer, killed it if they could, and came home; cavewomen wandered through the woods gathering whatever was out there. She says it's biology and that Darwin would understand better than I do."

"Zee is right, as usual," said Mattie.

"How's the backyard bridge project coming along?" asked John.

"Nearly there. You'll be invited to the grand opening."

As I drove away, I thought about the Mad Hatters. If Abigail Highsmith was one of the crazy members of that family, it was possible that she was, as John had suggested, the cause of Henry's almost unnatural irritation with me when we'd met at the fish market. Maybe her craziness had made him crazy and he had taken it out on me. Maybe her craziness also explained why she drove her bicycle off the road.

Maybe she was crazy enough to shoot her husband.

Hmmmm.

But John had told me that he'd never seen any sign that she was one of the Mad Hatters, and Joanne Homlish had sworn that a blue SUV that looked like mine had driven Abigail into the ditch, and someone besides Abigail had shot Abigail, so maybe she wasn't crazy at all. Maybe she was a sane Hatter, like most of them.

I went down into Edgartown and, because it was midafternoon and all of the sensible tourists were at the beach, I actually found a parking place on North Water Street, up toward the Harborview Hotel. Amazing but true.

I walked back to the library and once again dug out *Who's Who,* wherein I looked up Hatters and found very little other than that John had been right about the Hatter family's history of intellectual prominence and psychological peculiarities. Brimming with the confidence of the naive, I abandoned the book and went to the computer, where, amazingly enough, I was quickly able to find much more about the Hatters, which included descriptions of family oddness and left no doubt in a reader's mind that some of the Hatters were very strange birds whose lives were characterized by all sorts of idiosyncrasies, including episodes of violent psychosis. One of the latter, I noted, was apparently Abigail Highsmith's grandfather, who had been obliged to live out his last years under the care of a private doctor.

Mad Hatters indeed.

While I was there, I found Jasper Jernigan's bio and reviewed what I'd previously read about him, but at first saw nothing new as I wondered some more about why a millionaire golf addict would need a combination bodyguard and golf buddy. But then some lines caught my eye and I felt a little tingle somewhere in my psyche. I'd read them the first time I'd scanned Jasper's biography, but had thought nothing of them. Now, however, the simple information jumped at me. Jasper had married Helen Collins and was stepfather to her two children, who attended the prestigious Tuttle School.

Margy and Biff Collins attended the Tuttle School, where Biff was on the swimming team. Both of them had been at the beach party, and Biff was the boy who had gone off with Heather Willet and the young Highsmiths.

According to Belinda Highsmith, Biff had gone for a swim almost immediately after the foursome had left the rest of the party and hadn't swum back until after Heather had disappeared.

The warm sun was on my back when I left the library and walked to the Land Cruiser. The dreaded summer meter cop was working her way along the street in front of me, whistling as she ticketed cars, but I passed her and pulled away before she got to my spot.

I wanted to talk with Jasper Jernigan, but Jasper lived on Nantucket, so I drove to Glen Norton's house instead.

I hadn't seen him since we'd found Henry Highsmith's body, and I wondered, idly, if he'd been back to play golf at Waterwoods. I doubted it.

My doubts were justified.

"Hell, no," said Glen, after he'd put a glass in my hand and waved me out to a chair in his yard. "That business spooked me so much that I wonder if I can ever play out of a sand trap again. I haven't played a round since, at Waterwoods or anywhere else."

"Maybe what you need to do is go out on the beach and whack away at the sand until you're past the jitters. That Highsmith business was a once-in-a-lifetime thing, after all, and you'll never be happy until you're out on the course again."

"Yeah, you're right, but I'm not like you and Jasper and Gabe. You guys are all tougher than me, I guess. Hitting that hand shook me up pretty good!"

"Anybody would have been shaken," I said. Then I added, "Except for Gabe. He never seemed to blink an eye. What do you know about him, anyway?"

"Gabe? Not much. He works for Jasper and pals around with him all the time. I haven't seen them apart for the past several years, in fact. When Jasper plays, Gabe plays."

"Did you ever notice how Gabe's drives always go in the same area as Jasper's drives? How they never get too far apart on the fairways?"

Glen frowned at me. "I never thought about it, but now that you mention it, I guess that's right."

"Did you ever know Gabe to beat Jasper on any hole except one that was followed by a par-three hole? My impression was that Gabe's the better golfer, but that

day we played together I never saw him drive before
Jasper did except on that par-three fourth hole."

Glen squinted at me. "What are you getting at?"

"I noticed that Gabe always waited for Jasper to drive
first, then drove close to wherever Jasper drove. He had
to three-putt on the first two holes in order to stay
behind Jasper, but he won the third hole pretty easily
after Jasper got close to the green on his second shot.
Gabe drove first on the fourth hole and landed on the
green, but I'll bet you a nickel that he was going to lose
that hole to Jasper if we'd gotten a chance to play it."

Glen sipped his drink and frowned fiercely at his
glass.

"Why would he do that?"

"So he could see where Jasper's drive went off the
next tee before he made his own drive. He's good
enough to control his drives but he has to know where
Jasper drives so he can put his own ball pretty close to it
and give himself a reason to stay near Jasper. He
couldn't do that if Jasper was a pro, but Jasper's not a
pro and his drives are short. Did you ever notice that
Gabe carries a carbine or some sort of sawed-off rifle in
his golf bag?"

Glen's narrowed eyes widened. "Hell, no! Does he?
What are you telling me?"

"I think I'm telling you that Gabe is Jasper's bodyguard."

"Bodyguard?!"

"Gabe stays close to Jasper on the golf course and has
a rifle in case he needs one. That tells me that Jasper
has enemies. I'm hoping that you can tell me something
about them and maybe about Gabe."

"Good grief," said Glen, shaking his head. "I don't
know anything about any of this. I must be more naive
than I thought. No wonder I'm the only one of us

who's still spooked by that hand in the sand trap. I feel like Little Red Riding Hood in a forest full of wolves!"

"You don't have any idea about who might be interested in attacking Jasper?"

Glen had another drink from his glass. "No. I've read about celebrities surrounded by bodyguards and I know about the secret service and all that, but I never guessed that Jasper had his own guard."

"Jasper and Henry Highsmith tangled in the newspapers, and the exchanges got pretty hot. Did you ever hear Jasper actually threaten Henry or say that Henry had threatened him?"

"No! Never. I never heard him say any such thing. Are you trying to say that Jasper might have had something to do with Highsmith's murder? That's a crazy idea, J.W.!"

"I don't know if it's crazy," I said, "but it could well be wrong. The cops will be asking the same questions if they haven't done it already, though. What do you know about Jasper's family?"

"What do you mean?"

"I know he has a place on Nantucket. Did he fly over that day just to play with us at Waterwoods?"

"Yes, he did. He's got his own jet, so he flies to a lot of New England courses during the summer. Why?"

"He's married to a woman with two children by a previous marriage. Both kids go to school in Connecticut and both of them were at that beach party earlier this summer, when the Willet girl drowned. I'd like to talk with the boy. Do you know if he's staying somewhere here on the Vineyard?"

"That's one thing I do know," said Glen, who seemed glad to know something for a change. "All of Jasper's family are over on Nantucket. The kids came over here just for that party. Sort of a welcome-to-summer party with their friends, I think Jasper called it. Of course it turned out to be a terrible night and his kids went back to Nantucket as soon as the police were through talking with them. I think the boy is lifeguarding over there this summer. Why all these questions about Jasper and his family? They're fine people."

"The boy, Biff Collins, was one of the last people to see the girl alive. I'd like to hear what he has to say about what happened that night."

"The police already talked with him."

"I'd like to talk with him myself, and maybe you can help me out."

"How?"

"If I go over to Nantucket, I might run into a stone wall because Jasper and his family don't really know me. But you're Jasper's friend. If you call him and ask him to let me talk to him and his stepson, I might be able to ask them a few questions and get some answers."

"Is that why you came over here? To get me to grease the skids for you?"

"Do you mind?"

He thought about that for almost no time. "No. That's what friends are for: to help each other out if they can." He glanced at his Rolex. "I'll give Jasper a call. Tomorrow, okay?"

"The sooner the better. I'll fly over and take a taxi to his place."

Glen allowed himself the first smile I'd seen for a while. It was an ironic one. "You must really want to talk with those guys, J.W. You're usually pretty tight with your pennies, but here you are ready to shell out flying and taxi money. Wait here. I'll be right back." He walked into the house.

When he came out, he had good news for me. "Jasper says he and the boy will see you tomorrow morning. And you don't have to take that taxi. He'll meet you at the airport when you come in. Just give him a call when you know what flight you'll be on. You ever seen the new terminal at Nantucket?"

"I've never even seen the Nantucket airport."

"It's pretty snazzy. Let me know what you find out. You've got me wanting to know the real story."

I shook his hand. "I'll let you know. It's the least I can do. Meanwhile, find yourself a quiet beach and practice your wedge shots until you feel good enough to get back to the auld game."

I drove home and got to the end of our driveway just in time to see Joshua at our mailbox, pulling out envelopes and a newspaper. I offered him a ride down to the house.

"Did you see that guy, Pa?" he asked.

"What guy is that?"

"The guy at our mailbox. When I got up here to the road, he was parked there and was looking at the mail. When he saw me, he pushed the mail back in the box and drove away fast. Did you see him? It's against the law to steal mail!"

"Maybe he didn't steal anything, Josh. What did he look like?"

"He wasn't as old as you, but he was old."

Old, to anyone Joshua's age, could mean anyone between middle school age and the grave.

"What kind of a car was he driving?"

"An old one sort of like this one, only yellow."

"Yellow?"

"Yeah. You know. Sort of like a school bus only not quite. Why was he reading our mail?"

"I don't know. Maybe he was just at the wrong box."

"I think we should call the police!"

"I don't think the police can catch him now," I said. "Have any of those envelopes been opened?"

Joshua fingered through them. "Nope."

"What are they?"

He fingered again. "Two bills and a letter from Aunt Margarite and another one from Nana."

If the stranger had stolen anything, I couldn't imagine what it might have been. But I didn't think he was trying to steal anything, I thought he was verifying that the mailbox was mine and that I lived at the end of the driveway. I didn't like that at all.

— 24 —

I caught the early Cape Air flight to Nantucket about the same time that Zee and Mattie and their offspring headed for New Bedford. I was glad that Zee and the kids would be safely away all day. My flight time was only about twenty minutes, which meant that I could get to Nantucket quicker than I could drive to Aquinnah, and a lot faster than the shoppers would reach America.

There are many people on Martha's Vineyard who have been around the world but have never been to Nantucket, and vice versa, because they can see no reason to visit a neighboring island inferior to their own. I had been to Nantucket on my honeymoon, when Zee and I had sailed the *Shirley J.* over there after our wedding, but I hadn't seen much of the island on that occasion and knew little about it other than that it was even more pricey than the Vineyard and was longer on fog and shorter on trees.

I only knew one guy who lived there. He was a painter who long ago had bought a house and studio for what at that time had seemed an impossibly high price but now seemed like theft. Better yet, he'd managed to make enough money from his paintings to pay off his mortgage, so now he nestled comfortably on the outskirts of the village, painting and selling his work to castle builders, who didn't bat an eye at the prices he charged. What more could an artist ask?

Two centuries earlier, Nantucket had been a famous port for whaling ships, but then the canny Quaker boat owners, anxious for even more money, built ships too large to cross over the bar at the entrance to their harbor and thereby put Nantucket out of the whaling business. Thereafter, Edgartown and New Bedford, with their deep harbors, had become homes to the whaling ships and Nantucket had disappeared into the fog until its resurrection as a summer resort.

Nowadays, the tidal wave of money that was washing across Martha's Vineyard was even higher on the Gray Lady. People who couldn't afford to live on Nantucket built their mansions on Martha's Vineyard instead, and Nantucket workmen lived on Cape Cod and flew daily to and from their island work sites because it was cheaper to do that than to try to live on the island.

Thus I was not surprised by the fact that Jasper Jernigan, who summered on Nantucket, had his own private jet, or to verify, when we landed, that the terminal at the island's airport was as snazzy as advertised.

Jasper met me at the door as I walked out into the sunlight. He was accompanied, of course, by Gabe Fuller. Gabe didn't have his golf bag but was instead wearing a loose, bright-colored summer shirt that pretty well hid the bulge on his right hip. I shook both of their hands.

"I hope this is important," said Jasper. "I'd rather be playing golf than be here."

"Glen Norton can't bring himself to risk getting into a sand trap," I said. "He's still seeing that hand in the sand."

"Glen is a nice guy, but he's got to get a hold on himself."

We reached Jasper's car. It was a Hummer. Hummers were very fashionable that year. Gabe took the wheel and I climbed into the backseat. It was my first time in a Hummer, and I felt just a little bit like Arnold Schwarzenegger. Jasper, who was sitting in the suicide seat, turned to me as Gabe drove out of the airport. "Now, what's on your mind, J.W.?"

There was no point in being coy. "Two things. If you don't want to help me out, just turn around and take me back to the airport and I'll catch the next plane home. First, who's Gabe, here, and why does he carry a rifle in his golf bag? I don't think he's a regular member of the office staff."

Gabe, hearing these words, didn't swerve or speed up or slow down, but drove steadily and silently on.

Jasper looked me in the eye for a moment, then said, "When I was younger, my best friend was Carl Collins. He was married and had two little kids and a lot of money. Some people decided to kidnap him and collect a ransom. Things went wrong and Carl was killed. Do you know the story?"

"No, but I know you married a woman named Helen Collins who had two children."

"Carl's widow. I didn't want to put Helen through that again, so I hired Gabe. He's ex-FBI. I gave him a cover job at the office." He offered a slight smile. "His qualifications include being able to shoot straight and being willing to play a lot of golf."

If Gabe was ex-FBI, it wouldn't be too hard to get a line on what sort of agent he'd been, but I didn't want to wait, so I said, "The three of us here are of interest to the police in regard to the Highsmith shootings, because you and I tangled with Highsmith before his death and because Gabe might be the triggerman in case you didn't do the job yourself. I didn't hit him or his wife, but some people probably think I did, and I want to prove them wrong. Highsmith was shot the night before we found him. Where were you two when that happened?"

"You're pretty gutsy to ask a question like that of two guys who may be murderers," said Gabe. "You're a long way from home and you could have an accident before you get back." I lifted my eyes and saw his face grinning in the rearview mirror.

"Just call me Arnold," I said. "Where were you?"

"We were at the house here on the island," said Jasper. "We flew over to the Vineyard the next morning to play the round with you and Glen. My wife and the kids will tell you the same thing. I already told this to the cops."

"Yeah, but they didn't know about Gabe's rifle then. They do now and they'll want to talk with you again."

"And I'll tell them what I just told you. They can check everything: when we flew over that morning; whether my plane was on the ground the day before, and it was; whether I was playing golf here that previous afternoon, and I was; and whether my wife and children and I all had supper together that evening, and we did."

"That takes care of you. Where was Gabe?"

Again I saw Gabe's grin in the mirror. "Sounds like *This Gun for Hire,*" he said. "You think maybe I'm Alan Ladd?"

Old movies seemed all the rage. First *Tarzan and the Leopard Woman* and now *This Gun for Hire*. What next, O Lord? "You're about a foot taller than Alan," I said, "but I'd still like to know where you were."

"Gabe has an apartment in the east wing of the house," said Jasper. "He had supper with us."

"Beef Stroganoff," said Gabe. "Apple pie and ice cream for dessert."

"Patsy, the cook, is Gabe's wife," said Jasper, "and she

has a record of every meal she's cooked since she came to us with Gabe." He pointed ahead at a driveway. "You can ask her yourself in a minute."

We turned in and followed the winding drive to a huge house that overlooked Nantucket Sound. There was a practice green off to one side of the house and what looked like a tee and fairway just beyond it.

"Nine-hole, par-three course," said Jasper, following my gaze. "Mine. I wanted to make it bigger but my neighbor wouldn't sell me the land I needed. One of those Saudi sheiks with so much money he makes me look like a pauper. I couldn't budge him. You want to talk to Patsy and Helen? They'll verify that Gabe and I were right here when Highsmith got himself shot. And when his wife got shot, for that matter, in case you think we might have done that too."

I had come too far to say no, so I said yes, and he and Gabe took me to them and they did indeed verify that their husbands had been there on the fatal night.

It was possible, of course, that they'd gotten together on the story ahead of time just in case somebody like me showed up asking questions, but if so there'd be a record of Jasper's jet's arrivals and departures that would give the lie to the alibi, and I doubted if Jasper or Gabe was dumb enough to use a story that could be so easily disproved.

"You have any more questions about Gabe or me?" asked Jasper, good-humoredly. He didn't seem a bit put out by my inquiries, and my estimation of him went up accordingly.

"No," I said, "but I'd like to ask Biff a few things."

"Sure," he said. "He was going to shoot a round while I went to get you at the airport. He can't be far. Come on. You don't have to tag along, Gabe. We're not leaving the grounds."

"I can use the exercise," said Gabe, and the three of us started for the little golf course. Gabe walked beside me and said, "Another thing. I don't shoot a twenty-two. I know that it's popular and that probably more people get killed with that caliber than any other, but I like something a little bigger, something with more stopping power. You know what I mean?"

"Maybe you borrowed a twenty-two."

"I'd have borrowed, maybe, a forty-five."

"The twenty-two was enough to do the job. You have any ideas about who might have done it?"

He shook his head and sent his eyes ahead of us, sweeping them to the left and right. "No," he said, "I only know who didn't do it."

We topped a hill and I saw a lone figure ahead of us on a green, preparing for a putt.

"Kid's a real jock," said Jasper approvingly. "On the school swim team, the golf team, and the football team. He'd be on more teams, but the schedules overlap. He has school buddies out here sometimes to play this course and water-ski. Good student too, just like his sister."

I thought but didn't say that Biff liked a party too. Ahead of us, the boy two-putted, then saw us and waited until we reached him. I was introduced and he gave me a strong teenage hand. He was slope-shouldered and muscular and very polite with me, but comfortable at the same time, as young people sometimes are when they're used to being around adults.

"How's the round?" asked his stepfather.

"Three over," said the boy. "I missed some greens."

"J.W. says he wants to ask you some questions."

Biff looked at me with big blue eyes. "What about, Mr. Jackson?" Both his eyes and his voice were careful.

"Can we step away from you two," I asked Jasper and Greg, "or do you want to hear what we say?"

"I don't think Biff has any secrets from me," said Jasper, in a cooler voice than he'd been using.

"Everybody has secrets," I said. "I can do this either way, with you listening or not listening."

Jasper tried to be fair. "What do you prefer, Biff? You decide."

But Biff hedged. "I don't know. I can't think of any secrets. What do you want to ask, Mr. Jackson? What do you want from me?"

"I want to ask you about Gregory and Belinda High-smith and about what happened at the beach party that night."

"Wait a minute, now," said Jasper firmly. "The police have already talked with Biff about that night, and I don't want you bringing it up again or him thinking about it any more than he has to. I want him to put it behind him and move on."

"That's sensible," I said, "but the fact is that Biff may find himself a prime suspect in a murder case if he can't explain a few things."

Jasper's voice was as flat as Gabe Fuller's stare. "Murder case? What murder case? What are you talking about?"

"I'm talking about Heather Willet's death that night at the beach. Biff was one of the last people to see her alive. It wouldn't be too hard for a savvy prosecutor to make a case for him being the very last one."

"That was no murder; it was an accident!"

"Don't be so sure of that. The girl was found naked, with bruises on her head that may have been caused by blows with a rock. Biff, here, swam out into Vineyard Sound while Heather was still with the two Highsmith kids, and he didn't show up again until some time after Heather had left them. The Highsmiths say they were together after she left, but nobody knows where Biff was."

I looked at Biff. "I want to know where you were when Heather ran away from Gregory and Belinda Highsmith. What were you doing? What did you see? What did you hear?

Biff's voice lost its coolness. "I was swimming! I was far out. It was dark. I couldn't see anything. I didn't hear anything. When I got tired, I came in. Heather was gone. We looked for her but we couldn't find her, so we called the police. That's what happened! I told all this to the police!"

"Leave him alone," said Jasper.

"You must have been able to hear something," I said to Biff. "Gregory and Belinda said they could hear you calling for them to come out and join you, so you should have been able to hear them when they answered. And if you were close enough to shore to hear them, you were close enough to see Heather take off her bathing suit and go to Gregory. Did you see that? Did you see Gregory push her away? Did you see Heather run off alone?"

"No! I didn't see that! I couldn't see much. Maybe I heard them shout something. Maybe I caught a glimpse of Heather . . ."

"The police will wonder whether you followed her down the beach. She was a pretty girl and she was naked and you were all drinking, and the police will think it's possible that you wanted to have sex with her and she resisted and you hit her with a rock."

"No!" he blurted. "That never happened! I wasn't interested in Heather! I was interested in Belinda!" He looked at his stepfather, then at me, wishing, I suspected, that he'd curbed his tongue but knowing it was too late. He smiled a bitter smile. "I wanted Belinda to come swimming with me. I didn't care about Heather. It was Belinda. I've been after her for two years. What a joke."

"What are you talking about?" asked Jasper. "What do you mean?"

The boy looked at him almost scornfully. "You know those times we had Gregory over to play golf here and Belinda got invited because it made her unhappy to be left home while her brother came over here?"

Jasper nodded. "Yes. I remember. I thought you boys were pretty good about having a thirteen-year-old trail along after you."

"Well, she was the one I was interested in, not Gregory, and I've kept being interested in her even though she wasn't exactly trailing along with Gregory and me."

"What do you mean?"

"I mean she didn't want him out of her sight. Remember the time I asked Bitsy Farkin over so we'd have a foursome when we played?"

"I remember. I always thought Bitsy was a nice girl. I've wondered why she never came again."

"I can tell you that. When Bitsy saw Gregory she got the hots for him in about ten seconds, and when Belinda saw that she almost sprouted fangs and claws. She wouldn't let Bitsy get within ten feet of Gregory. Bitsy couldn't get away fast enough afterward."

My ears were standing up like a wolf's. "So Gregory and Belinda both play golf," I said.

Biff nodded. "That's right. Their father didn't approve, so I imagine they never told him, but they played. Especially while they were on the Vineyard and he was back in New Haven."

"And at the beach that night, you were still interested in Belinda and not in Heather?"

"That's right." He sneered at himself. "I'm a slow learner."

Little gears were turning in my brain. "What did you really see that night?"

He took a breath and let it out. When he spoke I had the impression that he was glad to rid himself of a burden that had been weighing on him. "You really want to know? I'll tell you, then. Dad, you're not going to be happy about this. It wasn't Gregory who pushed Heather away, it was Belinda. And when Heather was gone, Belinda and Gregory went down onto their beach blanket together and started taking off their bathing suits." He gripped his golf club hard with both hands and gazed at us with the cynicism of disillusioned youth. "I couldn't take it, so I swam out and stayed out as long as I could. When I came back they were in their suits again."

Jasper was incredulous. "Are you saying they were incestuous? Are you sure?"

Biff looked at him with cynical affection. "Maybe you could call it being siblings with benefits," he said almost gently. "Their parents knew about it. They were going to send Belinda to a special school in Switzerland this fall. She and Gregory didn't like that idea at all, but there was nothing they could do about it."

"Jesus," said Jasper, looking at Gabe. "I can't believe it."

Gabe shrugged and said nothing.

"And you never saw Heather again that night?" I asked Biff.

He shook his head. "I can't prove I didn't, but I didn't. I swam out as far as I could, and stayed out there as long as I could. I can't prove that, either, but that's what happened."

"Well," said Jasper, looking at me. "I don't know what to say."

"You don't have to say anything," I said, "but Biff should tell the police what he just told us. As for me, I think you can take me back to the airport." I looked at

Biff. "Tell the police. It might help them." Growing up can be hard, and I felt sorry for him. I felt sorry for the rest of us too, and thought of Margaret and Golden-grove unleaving.

25

I was back on the Vineyard again before noon, full of questions and speculations. My first stop was at the *Gazette* offices, where I found Susan Bancroft at her computer, energetically typing with two fingers.

"What's new?" she asked, without stopping her writing.

"Not too much," I said. "I just came by to find out if you know how Abigail Highsmith is doing."

Her flying fingers flew on. "This morning's report is that she's improving. Are you still on that case? If so, and if you learn anything, you'd damned well better give it to me before you give it to any other reporter. You owe me."

"I don't know anything worth printing," I said.

"Then thank you for nothing and good-bye. If you do learn something I want first dibs."

"How many old yellow SUVs would you say are on the island?"

"How in blazes should I know? You ask some odd questions, McGee."

"I'm an odd guy," I said. "Type well."

I went out and drove to Dom Agganis's office, but it was Dom's turn to be out and Olive Otero's to be at the desk. Inwardly, I groaned.

But Olive was unexpectedly friendly. "Just the man I want to see. Ever since you mentioned *Tarzan and the Leopard Woman* I've had an itch to watch it again. I loved that movie when I was a kid, but I can't seem to find a copy of it anywhere. You know where I can get the video?"

Taken by surprise, I said, "I've got the only video I know of. I'll loan it to you."

Both Olive and I then stared at one another in silence, stunned by our own words.

Olive seemed to recover first. She shuffled some papers on her desk and cleared her throat and said, "That will be fine. Thank you. Now, what brings you here? Something about the Highsmith case, if I know you."

My voice sounded flat: "You should be able to get these same stories from Jasper Jernigan and his stepson, a boy named Biff Collins, but in case either one of them changes his mind about that, here's what they told me today." I told her what I'd been told on Nantucket.

Olive got out a tape recorder and said, "Do you mind repeating that?"

I didn't mind, and when I was through, Olive put the tape machine back in its drawer.

"I want Dom to get that straight from you instead of filtered through me," she said. "He's already planning to interview Jernigan and Gabe Fuller again. I don't know if what the Collins boy told you has any importance to the case, but it sounds like Dom will want to talk with him again too. Maybe we can put the screws to them all and learn more." She stared at me. "You got anything else?"

"Yes. I don't know what to make of it, but maybe it's important." I told her about the Shelkrotts' sudden departure from the Highsmith home.

She made a note and looked down at it. "I think Dom will be interested in this too, although it may mean nothing." She lifted her eyes. "You have any ideas?"

"Just the obvious ones: they're on the run from the law or they can't take the pressure in the household and decided to pull out before the stress kills them."

"Do you think they're on the lam?"

I felt myself frowning. "When I talked with them they didn't seem the kind of people who would just cut and run. They'd been with the family for a long time, through thick and thin."

"What, then?"

"I don't know. I think it's very odd."

"There are a lot of odd people in the world. In this business we meet more than our share of them. If the Shelkrotts are still on the island, maybe we can find them. If they went back to the mainland, maybe we can find out where. You got anything else to put on my plate?"

"No, but there's a chance you can help me. How many old yellow SUVs do you think there are on this island?"

"I have no idea. Do you?"

"No, but I know that Heather Willet's parents own one. It's parked up in their barn."

"How do you know what's in their barn?" Her eyes narrowed a bit.

"Because I saw it there when I went to talk with them."

"The Willets are in Michigan, as far as I know."

"I know that now, but I didn't know it then."

"Why the question about old yellow SUVs?"

I told her about the yellow SUV that Joshua had seen.

Olive listened politely, then said, "So what? Guy probably just stopped at the wrong mailbox. Didn't steal anything, so there was no crime. What's your beef?"

It was a pretty feeble beef, when looked at objectively. "An old SUV ran Abigail Highsmith off the road, according to Joanne Homlish, and Joanne says it looked like mine, but it wasn't. The one Joshua saw was yellow, but Joshua says it looked like mine otherwise."

Olive counted on her fingers. "So you have two cases of old SUVs that look like yours but aren't, and you have another old yellow one up in the Willets' barn. Is that it? There are dozens of rusty old SUVs on this island, J.W. Go home and get out that video for me. Is it okay if I come by and pick it up?"

"Come any time," I said, getting up from my chair. "I'll leave it out for you, in case I'm not there."

But I didn't go home; I drove to the Willet place, parked in front of the barn, and peeked through the window. The old yellow SUV was there, but it didn't seem to be quite in the same place as before.

I backed off and studied the gravel drive. There, faintly, I could see what looked like indentations made by tires that led to the big barn door.

I went to the barn door and looked closely at the padlock. It was a heavy lock snapped onto a hasp that looked strong enough to resist Samson.

I went to the house and knocked on the front door, then circled the house, calling hello to anyone who might be there. No one was. I returned to the barn and circled it, calling some more but finding no one. I looked up at the field on the slope behind the barn, where the trail led to the Highsmith place. No one was in sight.

I got out my lock picks and was inside the barn before you could say rubber baby buggy bumpers.

The barn was an echo chamber, magnifying every sound. It was clean, as barns go, and was being used mostly to store the sort of stuff that you have but rarely if ever use, but don't want to get rid of just in case you or someone you know might want or need it someday: furniture in need of paint, boxes, tools, outgrown toys and games, and farm implements, including a plow, a harrow, and a riding lawn mower. And the old yellow Mitsubishi Pajero SUV.

I went to the truck and tried the door. Unlocked. I climbed into the cab and found the ignition keys in the glove compartment. The Willets apparently trusted the big padlock on the barn door and presumed that local thieves lacked both lock picks and crowbars.

A lot of Vineyarders are even more trusting, including me. I almost never lock either my car or my house doors, although I do make it a policy not to leave my keys in my car. Those islanders who do leave their keys in the ignition usually believe that since they live on an island, there's no place to go in a stolen car and therefore no reason to fear car thieves. They get their cars stolen just often enough to make the rest of us feel intelligent, usually by some kid or drunk or by someone who, just for thrills or laughs, drives it into a tree or into some pond.

I got out of the truck and left the barn, locking the big door behind me. I picked the lock on the kitchen door of the house and went into the kitchen, where most people keep keys behind a closet or cabinet door. I found the Willets' supply in the broom closet and took them back to the barn, where I quickly found the one that opened the padlock. I relocked the padlock, returned the keys to the closet, and took a quick tour of the house. On the second floor, overlooking the front porch, I found what looked like a teenage girl's bed-room. Heather's room.

I spent a half hour carefully looking in bureau draw-ers, under the mattress, under the bed, in the closet, and behind mirrors and framed prints of fatigued-looking young people I presumed were rock stars unknown to me. I found nothing of interest and left, leaving everything as I had found it. If Heather had ever had a photo of Gregory Highsmith, it was no longer in evidence. Neither was a diary detailing her sex life.

Peeks through several upstairs windows revealed no one in sight; still, when I left the house and drove away, I could feel eyes on my back. Did I feel guilty about being a housebreaker? I was reminded of Byron's rue-ful comment that his religious upbringing didn't pre-vent him from sinning but did prevent him from enjoying it as much as he might have.

The view from the Willet place was of green hills, a green pasture on the other side of North Road, and the blue Atlantic in the distance. There were red cattle grazing near a blue pond in the pasture, and a white farmhouse on the far side of it. Arching over all of this was a pale blue sky holding a sun too bright to look at. No wonder people wanted to live on Martha's Vine-yard.

Blue water, blue sky, red cattle, a white farmhouse, green trees and grass. Color everywhere. I remem-bered the reading I'd done as preparation for helping Joshua write his paper on the color wheel, and then remembered the yellow and blue window trim at Joanne Homlish's house, and immediately wondered why I hadn't linked those things before.

One of the most annoying and unanswerable ques-tions in the world must be "Why didn't you think of that before?" Who can possibly know why he didn't think of something that afterward seems so obvious? But the fact is that it happens all the time; we think of some things but not others. Maddening.

I drove to West Tisbury and followed Tiah's Cove Road to Joanne Homlish's house. A large white-haired man was in front of the barn with an ax in his hand. He gave me a benign look as I approached him. I told him my name and asked if he was Marty Homlish.

"That's me," he said, shaking hands. "I don't think we've met."

"We haven't, but I was here a few days ago and had a talk with your wife."

"Joanne's gone to the store. Should be back soon."

"I may not have to see her. Tell me, who painted the trim around those lower windows? Did your wife do it?"

He followed my gaze and laughed. "You guessed it. I did the second-floor trim, using the ladder, and Joanne did the lower trim. Just last year. But you can see how hers turned out. Some blue and some yellow. I should repaint it this year."

"I noticed it the last time I was here," I said, "but it didn't sink in. She's color blind, isn't she?"

"Yep. Blue-yellow. Pretty rare condition. Most color-blind people can't tell the difference between green and red, but Joanne mixes up blue and yellow. I've talked with her about it, but I still don't know what, exactly, she sees when she's looking at those colors. Some kind of gray, I think. I don't know how she decides what the real color is, but she didn't do a very good job of it on that trim." He laughed again.

"Why didn't she just read the color off the cans?"

"I asked her the same thing. Turns out she used old cans where the paint had slopped over the side and covered the words. My doing, of course. When I paint I get more on my clothes than on what I'm supposed to be painting. Drives Joanne wild, because she never spills a drop. I tell her that at least I know blue from yellow, but that doesn't mollify her a bit."

"My truck there is blue," I said. "Are you saying that if it was yellow, she couldn't tell the difference?"

He nodded. "You got it. You want to talk with her about it, she should be home in a half hour or so. "

"No," I said. "I don't need to see her. Just tell her I came by to say hello."

"I'll do that," said Marty. He lifted his ax. "You aren't interested in splitting a little wood, are you?"

"Not right now."

"I didn't think so. I try to do a little at a time so next winter I'll have all I need. I'm getting too old to swing an ax all day like I used to do."

"I know what you mean," I said, "You must have heard the joke about the guy who was complaining about his sex life."

"I know the one," said Marty. "Said it took him all night long to do what he used to do all night long. That the one?"

"That's the one."

"The problem is, it ain't no joke," said Marty, with a grin.

I drove back home, thinking that things were falling into place.

At the head of our driveway I stopped at the mailbox and found junk mail, including a medium-size pile of catalogs selling everything imaginable. I claim that Zee is the catalog queen of Martha's Vineyard, but men I know say that she's no match for their wives. I've wondered from time to time how much money has been spent on mailing catalogs. Less than has been brought in by them, apparently, since there seem to be more of them every day.

I was halfway down our driveway when I saw ahead of me, parked in front of our house, an old yellow SUV. I felt a chill in spite of the warm summer sun.

26

Our driveway is narrow and sandy, and there are trees and oak brush on both sides of it, but there are places to turn off if you know where they are and you don't mind a few more scratches on your car. My old Land Cruiser was beyond caring about more cosmetic damage, so I pulled off the drive and parked under a big oak tree.

I got out and circled toward the house, moving slowly and trying to look everywhere at once. When the house came into view, I slowed still more, then stopped to study both it and the yellow SUV parked in front of it, looking for movement.

There was no doubt about it; the SUV was the rusty Mitsubishi Pajero I'd seen in the Willets' barn. But where was the driver? Who was the driver? I could see no one.

I curved deeper into the woods then circled back behind the shack at the rear of the house. The shack has a woodstove, and I clean scallops there in the fall and winter when it's too cold to clean them outside. I also kept tools in there, but, alas, none was a firearm. Maybe I should stick one of my father's old shotguns out there, just in case. Too late now.

I peered around the corner of the shack and studied the back of the house. Bedroom windows and the kitchen door stared back silently. Was someone inside studying me as I studied the house?

I waited, saw nothing, and then trotted to the kitchen door. I tried the screened door. It opened without a squeak. Good old WD-40. I stood straight and peeked through the small window in the inner door. I could see the kitchen and through the far door leading to the living room. Beyond that I saw the front door swinging shut as someone went out onto the screened porch in front of the house and shut the door behind him (her?).

I opened the door and went into the kitchen, holding my breath and walking softly in case some other intruder had stayed behind. Our master bedroom was immediately on my left and the door was open. I sneaked a quick look inside, saw nothing, and stepped in.

No one. I breathed again, and then listened. Nothing.

I went back into the kitchen, listening hard and avoiding the squeaky board in front of the stove as I went to the door to the living room.

Outside, a motor started, and when I glanced across the room I saw through a window that the yellow Mitsubishi was moving toward the driveway.

I couldn't see the driver. Should I plunge across the room and hope to get a glimpse of him or her at the risk of making myself an unmissable target if the driver had an accomplice still inside the house?

Caution or cowardliness prevailed. While the sound of the SUV's motor grew fainter, I swept the living room with my eyes and saw no one. Only two bedrooms and the bathroom to go. I crept into them one by one and found no one.

I went to the gun case, snagged the key from its top, unlocked it, and got out the old .38 police revolver I'd used when I was a Boston cop, before the days when the police began carrying Glocks and Berettas in hopes of matching the bad guys in firepower. I filled the cylinder and shoved the gun under my belt.

I went through the house again just to be sure, looking as I did so for signs the intruder might have left behind. I found only an empty Sam Adams bottle on the floor beside a living room chair. My guest had gotten thirsty while waiting for me. At least he or she had good taste in beer. I sat in the chair and found myself looking directly at the front door. I pointed my forefinger and said, "Bang."

I walked outside and looked up at the tree house. What the hell? I climbed up and verified that it was empty. My visitor obviously had never seen *Tarzan and the Leopard Woman* or he or she would have gone up there to admire my construction and then stayed there because of the good view he or she had of anyone coming into the yard. Although I'd never noticed it before, the tree house was an excellent shooting station.

But maybe the driver wasn't a shooter. Maybe he or she wanted to see me for some other reason. I had no basis to think otherwise.

But I did think otherwise.

I swung down to the ground on the rope hung for that purpose and walked up the driveway to my truck. Had my visitor noticed it off there under the oak? If so, what had he or she thought?

It was annoying to constantly use the phrase "he or she." Why couldn't English have a good gender-free singular pronoun for a human? The plural pronouns were all that way, why not the singular ones?

I backed carefully to the driveway and then drove down to the house. I was worried. What if Zee and the children had been home when the driver of the Mitsubishi had arrived? Would they have been in danger? The thought angered and frightened me. I added up all that I had seen and heard having to do with the Highsmith business, added it again, then went into the house and called Dom Agganis. I got Olive Otero.

"You again," she said. "What is it this time?"

I told her what had passed since last we'd talked, and said, "I think we should go up to Chilmark and find out who's been driving that yellow Mitsubishi."

"You think Willet may have sneaked back here when we thought he was in Michigan?"

"What I know about him is that he has a twenty-two target pistol, he has a gripe against the Highsmiths, and he owns a truck that might have run Abigail Highsmith off the road."

"I'm going to make a couple of calls," said Olive. "I don't want you going up there alone. Come here instead."

"I should probably stay here in case that driver comes back."

Her voice was firm. "No. I want to know where you are and what you're doing, so come here. I'll try to get search warrants for the Willet place and the Highsmith place, and I'll get Dom and the Chilmark police here for a strategy meeting. You can tell them what you know and we'll decide what to do. No solo heroics, J.W. You'll just get in our way."

"All right," I said. "I'll be right up."

It took a while for the interested parties to gather and for Olive to find a judge who would issue search warrants, but midafternoon the meeting got started. One of the Chilmark cops was the young officer who'd directed me to the Highsmith house the other day. He looked at me with interest.

"You first," said Dom, pointing a sausage-size finger at me. "Start from the beginning and stick to the facts."

I did that, going from my scuffle with Henry Highsmith to my near encounter with the driver of the yellow Mitsubishi at my house. When I was through, Dom asked, "What else do we have?"

What else they had were their interviews with every-one involved in the case and a couple of other bits: the Shelkrotts' car had not left the island, and, something of interest to me in particular, the Willets actually were still in Michigan.

That took most but not all of the steam out of the theory that Willet was the murderer.

"Maybe Willet hired somebody to do his work," said the young Chilmark cop. "Gave him the keys and the pistol and turned him loose."

"Is Willet that dumb?" objected an older Chilmark officer. "I don't think you hire somebody to use your car and your gun to kill somebody. It's not something I'd do."

"People do strange things," said Olive, "and we have some odd birds in this case."

"Willet might have been working with a loose screw after his daughter died. Maybe he wasn't thinking straight."

"If the Shelkrotts' car didn't leave the island, where is it? And where are they?"

"Car could be anywhere. Maybe they put it in the park-and-ride lot and went to America on foot."

"Why would they do that?"

A shrug. "Why did they take off in the first place?"

"What we'll do," said Dom, after listening to as much of such speculation as he could stand, "is go up there with our warrants and see what we can find. I want the Mitsubishi taken as evidence, which means you'll wear gloves when you touch it and that we'll need a truck and trailer to take it away. Olive . . ."

"I've already called the garage," said Olive. "They'll be ready for us when we're ready for them."

"We want the gun," said Dom, "so keep your eyes open." He described his plan, then looked around. "Any questions?"

There are always questions, the best one this time being, "Should we wear vests?"

"I always wear a vest," said Dom. "Yes, you should wear a vest. This is a murder investigation and we don't know what we're going to find up there."

"How about me?" I asked. "Do I get a vest?"

Dom frowned. "I don't think you'll need one since you're not going with us."

"I might be handy," I said. "I know where the key to the Willets' barn is, for instance."

"Bolt cutters will do the job just as well."

"I'd like to be in on the end of this business."

"This may not be the end of it."

"I'm a citizen and I can go where I please."

"I don't know if it pleases you to go to jail, but that's where I can put you right now."

"What's the charge?"

"Interfering with police officers doing their job."

I held both palms up in front of me. "Interfere? Not me. I promise not to even get close to Chilmark." I looked at the other officers. "You can witness that I promise not to interfere in any way. Dom, you can't arrest me for something I haven't done and won't do."

"What a terrible liar you are," said Dom. "How about for loitering, then?" His cop smile lacked warmth, I thought.

"How about letting me tag along instead? You owe it to me. If it wasn't for me you wouldn't be going up there."

Dom pursed his lips, then said, "Oh, all right. I guess it can't hurt. But stay out of the way when we get there. Olive, where'd I put that extra vest of mine? Oh, yeah, I remember." He went to a closet and groped around, then came up with an old vest and tossed it to me. It was heavy.

"This weighs a ton," I said, slipping it on. "Don't you have one of those fancy new ones like you're wearing?"

"That one's fine." Dom looked around and said, "Okay, we'll do it as we agreed. Two cars up to the Highsmith place and the other two to the Willets'. No sirens or lights. Olive, call the garage and have their truck and trailer follow us. Everybody ready? All right, let's go. And be careful. There's a murderer out there somewhere and we may be getting close to him. J.W., you ride with me."

We went out and climbed into the cruisers and drove through Vineyard Haven and on to points west. Dom's big fingers tapped the wheel as he drove.

"Do you buy the idea that the Willets hired a gun to do their work?" he asked.

"Most people don't know any gunmen or how to find one," I said. "The Willets might have been out of their minds with grief, but I don't think they'd have hired the first guy they asked."

"Maybe they'd been chewing on the idea for a long time and had already made their plans. Maybe the girl's death just triggered the plan."

"It's possible."

"But you don't like it."

"No. Do you?" I asked.

"No. An arranged hit is usually a straightforward murder or one that's supposed to look like an accident. The Highsmith killing was like a smart-ass stunt."

I nodded. "You mean the sand trap business. I agree. That's been odd from the beginning. It's sophomoric."

"There's something childish about most criminals," said Dom. "A lot of them can't read and according to Kohlberg, a lot of them never get past a kid's level of moral development."

I arched my brows. "Jeez, Dom. Is Kohlberg required reading in cop college these days? I didn't know you guys were so up on theories of morality."

"There's a lot you don't know, J.W. In your day, you boys in blue weren't reading anything more complicated than Spider-Man, but times have changed." He was silent for a moment, then he said, "Are you thinking what I'm thinking?

"I probably am," I said.

27

Dom was on the radio, again advising the occupants of the other cruisers to be especially careful. I had a slight headache as I ran things back and forth through my mind. Our caravan wound its way along State Road to North Tisbury, then hooked left at the old oak and right on Panhandle Road and went on into Chilmark. The westering summer sun was in our eyes and we squinted against it.

We came to the Highsmith driveway and Dom turned onto it, followed by one of the Chilmark cruisers. The other two cruisers and the truck and trailer went on to the Willet place.

The Volvo was parked in front of the garage. We stopped and got out of the cruisers.

"Careful, now," said Dom.

"There's an apartment over the garage," I said.

"Larry, you and Zim go check that out," said Dom. "If you find anybody, ask them to step outside. There should be at least three people living here. I've got the search warrants with me if anybody asks. Stay here, J.W."

He started for the house, but before he got there the front door opened and Gregory and Belinda Highsmith came out into the bright sun. Their arms were linked. They looked like a pair of angels. His white short-sleeved shirt hung over tan shorts; she was wearing a diaphanous white dress that was lightly tied at the waist and her long hair was down. She could have been stepping from a Pre-Raphaelite painting.

They looked at us, wide-eyed. "Officers, what are you doing here?"

Dom said, "We have a warrant to search this property. We'll appreciate your cooperation."

"I don't understand," said the boy in his musical baritone. "What are you looking for?"

"I want you two to stay here with Mr. Jackson," said Dom. "Where's your uncle?"

"Oh," said the girl, "I think he took a walk. He should be back soon."

"Step down here, please," said Dom. "This is the warrant. It allows us to search both the property and the people we find here. I'm going to start with you two. You first, young man. Put your hands here on the car."

"Shouldn't we have a lawyer?" asked the girl airily.

"It's too late for a lawyer to stop this search," said Dom. He patted Gregory down and found nothing that interested him. "You're next, miss."

Her angel eyes had been floating around the yard, watching Larry and Zim disappear into the garage, eyeing me with a vague contempt, watching Dom search her brother.

"I don't want your hands on me," she said to Dom in a suddenly icy voice.

He nodded. "A policewoman is at the Willet house. I'll have her come up."

"Never mind," she said, her voice switching smoothly to silk. She lifted her arms over her head and stepped so close to him that their bodies touched. "You do your duty, Officer. You'll probably like it a lot."

Her arms rose higher, seemingly to circle his neck, but then suddenly she drove her nails toward his eyes.

He jerked his head back and her nails raked down his cheeks before he could catch her wrists. She screamed an oath and tried to knee him as she writhed in his arms.

As if on command, the boy leaped forward and reached for Dom's holstered pistol, but I caught his arm. He had a mad strength and pushed me away, then lunged for the pistol again.

"Get it! Get it!" screamed Belinda. "Shoot them! Shoot them!"

I yanked my pistol out of my belt and laid the barrel hard on Gregory's arm. He cried out in pain and struck out at me with his other fist. My world turned dark, but I blocked his next blow and hit him hard in the face with the pistol. He fell down and blood began to flow from his broken nose. He put his hands to his face and began to cry.

"Coward! Coward! Oh, you coward! What have you done?" Belinda's voice was a feral howl, like that of the last wolf in the world. Dom pushed her away and she fell on her knees and cradled Gregory's head in her arms. "Gregory, what have they done to you? Oh, Gregory!"

There was blood on Dom's face, but he ignored it. Zim and Larry, having heard the howl, came out of the garage, guns in hand. They came running over.

"Cuff these two and put them in the cruiser," said Dom. "Take the boy to the hospital first, then take both of them to jail. Assaulting an officer will do for the time being. Watch yourselves every second. They're a couple of vipers."

"You stink!" screamed the girl. "All of you stink!" Zim snapped cuffs on her and pulled her to the cruiser, but she never stopped talking. "You don't belong here! You can't prove anything! You don't have any evidence at all! You're just stupid cops! We can hire the best lawyers in the world and they'll make you all look like fools! You *are* fools! I'm thirteen years old! Nothing will happen to us! We're just kids! You leave Gregory alone, damn you all! I'll kill you all!" She said more, but I had stopped listening.

Larry cuffed Gregory and I helped drag him to the cruiser. With Gregory and Belinda in the rear seat, he and Zim drove away.

I got the first aid kit from Dom's cruiser and cleaned up his face a little. "Better have somebody else look at this," I said. "That girl is so poisonous that she may have toxic nails."

"Later," he said. "Well, I'm shorthanded and you used to be a cop, so you can help me search this place. Afterward we'll get more people over to do a more thorough job. The girl may be right, you know. We may not have evidence that will hold up in court. We need the gun."

But we didn't find it. All we found was emptiness.

"If I was one of the kids," I said, "I wouldn't keep the gun here. I'd keep it someplace else." I looked out a back window of the house.

"If it's Willet's gun," said Dom, "why not keep it at Willet's house, right where Willet left it? That way they can claim to know nothing about it, especially if they wiped it clean afterward. Let's go down and give Olive a hand."

"First, look at this," I said. Dom came and stood beside me. I pointed. "That's the old road that used to lead to the rock quarry up on the hill. The grass looks bent down to me, as if somebody has driven a car up there."

"Yes, it does," said Dom. "We'll go there first."

We walked up the hill, following the faint imprint of

tires, until we crossed the top of the hill. There, a few yards beyond the crest, we came to the lip of the old quarry and looked down at the dark, quiet waters that filled the crater.

The tire tracks ended at the granite ledge on which we stood. I knelt and gestured at fresh scratches and a bit of blue paint on the stone.

"The Shelkrotts drove a blue Chevy station wagon," I said. I tried to see down through the quiet water, but it was too deep for my eyes, just as it had been too deep for the young Chilmark cop when he'd tried to find the bottom as a boy.

"We'll get divers and a crane up here," said Dom. "If we find what I think we'll find, we may not need that pistol after all." He stood up and looked around. "Where do you think we'll find Tom Brundy? Did the kids kill him too?"

"I don't know. That's his Volvo down there at the house. Maybe you should look in the trunk."

We went back down to the house. Dom got into the cruiser and began to make calls on his radio. Soon the place would be crawling with policemen. I was leaning against the car when Dom got out.

"I guess it's an old story," I said, "but I hate to think that kids will murder their parents."

"But you think this pair killed both the Willet girl and their father," said Dom, in a surprisingly gentle voice.

"One of them or both of them, yes. I don't know if it can ever be proved, but that's what I think. I think the kids are both Mad Hatters. While they were little, maybe no one saw that they were different from normal children, but as they grew older their parents and the Shelkrotts must have noticed they were strange. Then, when they reached puberty, they got interested in each other sexually and it became impossible to ignore. I believe that's why Henry Highsmith was so testy that day in the fish market. He was a man with two insane, incestuous children and he didn't know what to do about them. The only thing he could think of was to split the kids up by sending Belinda to school in Switzerland. It was the incest that drove the Willets away. They didn't want their daughter to associate with the crazy Highsmith children. Belinda said that it was the Highsmiths who cut off the relationship, but it was really the other way around."

"But the Willet girl still had the hots for Gregory," said Dom. "And when she made a play for him on the beach, they killed her. Is that it?"

"I'd lay my money on Belinda as the killer. She's nasty when any girl gets close to her brother. I see Gregory as the aider and abettor. I think it was a spur of the moment thing. They saw their chance to make it look like an accident, and they took it."

"After making out together on the beach."

"Yes. Maybe Heather came back and found them. Maybe that's what triggered the murder. We'll have to ask them about that."

"And you think it was Gregory, driving the Willets' old SUV, who ran his mother off the road."

"Yes. I think they decided that if they were going to stay together, they'd have to get rid of their parents, and that was their first try. The kids used to drive that old truck around the field behind the Willets' house. Every farm kid in the country learned to drive like that. The Willets had left the island, but the kids had a key to the house—my guess is that Gregory got it from Heather when she was trying to lure him into her arms—and got the padlock key from the closet. He knew his mother was riding her bike to Vineyard

Haven that day and he went after her and he almost got her. Afterward, she said it was her fault, but if she recognized the yellow truck, she must have had a different suspicion.

"Can you imagine what it must feel like to suspect that your child is trying to murder you?"

"You must go through a lot of denial," said Dom. Cops see such denial pretty often when they arrest some kid. The mother can't believe it and calls the cops bad names, even if she knows the kid's guilty.

I went on: "I figure Willet left his pistol in his house and that the kids got their hands on it about that time, probably after snooping through the place. Maybe they had it before, but didn't decide to use it until after they failed with the truck. Their chance came when their father was making his daily round-trip ride down-island. One of them, or maybe both of them, met him down there somewhere and shot him. It was dusk, too dark for anybody to be playing golf, so they took the utility road into Waterwoods and buried the body in that sand trap as a final snub. I'm willing to bet that if you check the records at Waterwoods, you'll find out that one or both of them played there at one time or another."

"A juvenile trick. Insult to injury."

"Also a pretty stupid thing to do because they were lucky not to have been seen. But they're kids, remember, and not as smart as they think they are."

"None of us are," said Dom. "Then they ambushed their mother when she came out of the funeral parlor. They went out ahead of her and saw another one of those moments of opportunity and took advantage of it. If the manager had come out with her, they might not have shot."

"Or they might have shot them both. If Abigail lives,

it'll be interesting to learn if she saw the shooter. A lot could depend on that, if this comes to trial."

"If she'll tell the truth," said Dom. "If she does that and if we find the pistol, we'll probably have a case. If we don't, we might not."

I left him there to deal with arriving policemen and walked down to the Willets' place.

The big barn door was open and the old yellow Mitsubishi was already on the trailer. Olive Otero and the two Chilmark policemen were in the house. I went in carefully, so as not to disturb anything. A lot of crime scenes are contaminated by the people investigating them, and I didn't want to be one of them. I didn't see anything different than I'd seen during my earlier, illegal entry, so I went out again and waited in the afternoon sun, feeling weary.

After some time, Olive came out, carrying an evidence bag. In the past, she wouldn't have given me the time of day, but this time she said, "Twenty-two Colt Woodsman and a couple of boxes of shells, one half empty. Smells like it's been fired recently. Looks wiped to me, but the lab will know. May be something on the magazine."

Could be. More than one not-so-clever shootist has wiped his prints off the murder weapon but has forgotten that he's left prints on the magazine. In any case, things seemed to be falling into place for the police.

Too late for Heather Willet and for Henry Highsmith, of course; too late for all of the Highsmiths, for that matter, and for the Shelkrotts too, if my fears about their fate were confirmed. And too late, too, for Tom Brundy. The world could be a dark place.

But I was wrong about Brundy. He came walking out of the woods while Dom Agganis was talking with the cops who were accumulating on the scene, and was first curious, then angry, then astonished, then aghast, and then in a state of near collapse, when he heard what Dom had to say.

I was relieved and surprised that he was still alive, but suspected that he wouldn't have survived too much longer if we hadn't showed up. Gregory and Belinda had, I thought, killed so many people already that one more would mean nothing to them.

That was yet to be proved in court, of course. They were very young and very sly and they had a lot of money. Circumstantial evidence might get them into a courtroom, but that evidence might be more impressive to me than to a jury. And even if the evidence was persuasive, there was their youth, especially Belinda's, to be taken into consideration, and there was always an insanity plea, for which they might well be qualified. All in all, I had my doubts that Gregory and Belinda would spend much time in the gray bar hotel. A better bet was that they'd be put into a comfortable hospital from which they stood a good chance of being released at age twenty-one.

The prospect did not please me, because it meant that I'd be looking over my shoulder for the rest of my life in case they came calling.

I wondered if the police would now look back farther into their lives and discover other unsolved killings that had occurred near Highsmith territory; the death of a playmate, for example, or of a neighbor's child. Would they learn that Gregory enjoyed pulling the wings off flies, or that Belinda's kitten had been found strangled, hanging from a tree?

Or had the killing begun with Heather Willet and then accelerated from there? And if so, could anyone ever prove it?

Was I right to suspect that Henry and Abigail Highsmith's plan to separate their children, to send Belinda
to that special school in Switzerland, had led the kids to
wish their parents dead? Was parental disapproval of
their incestuous love enough motive for murder? Or
did Gregory and Belinda have more powerful urges?
What was it that Gregory had said to me only two days
earlier: that all it takes is a sudden impulse? Were they
merely the latest Mad Hatters? If so, their madness, like
most, would be easier to describe than to explain. I
foresaw dueling psychologists in any Highsmith trial to
come.

One thing only was certain: the Highsmiths had been
an unhappy family, and Tolstoy had been right as usual
when he wrote that every unhappy family is unhappy
in its own fashion.

I was tired of being there, and got a Chilmark cop to
give me a ride back to the state police barracks, where
my truck was parked. He was talkative all the way, and
was eager to be back at the Highsmith place so he could
watch when the divers and the crane started work at the
stone quarry. It was the most exciting day he'd had
since joining the force. As soon as he let me out, he sped
away, heading back up-island.

It wouldn't be long before there would be reporters
on the scene, so I used the cell phone in the truck to call
Susan Bancroft and make sure she'd be among the
first. "Just keep your tipster's name to yourself," I said.

"My lips are sealed," she replied. "Thanks. I'm on
my way!"

I drove home, taking my time. When I got there, I
made myself a drink and climbed up to the balcony. I
looked across the garden to Sengekontacket Pond and
saw three swans swimming in a mini-flotilla. Beyond the
pond, sunbathers were still leaving the barrier beach

and heading home. Beyond them, on the blue waters of Nantucket Sound, sails were leaning across the wind.

I switched my gaze to the tree house and the almost completed rope bridge. I could probably finish that in half a day. I sipped my drink and wished my family were with me. No matter, they'd be home soon. When my glass was empty, I went down to the kitchen and began to put supper together. Zee and the kids would have a lot to tell me about their day in the big city, and I wanted to hear it all.

28

Three days later Olive Otero came by to pick up the video. By then, Joshua and Diana and five or six of their very best friends had spent considerable time scrambling around the tree house and the completed rope bridge to the oak tree, and had pronounced them good. Their next plan was for me to build a collapsible bamboo shower so they could swing on a rope and kick it over onto an attacking leopard man just like Boy did in the movie. All they really lacked was some actual or pretend leopard men to fight. I said I didn't think I was going to build a bamboo shower, and I didn't think that any of them should be leopard men because someone was sure to get hurt.

Olive Otero was also very impressed with the tree house and bridge, and to my slight surprise accepted Diana's invitation to come up and see things firsthand. She sat in the tree house, climbed around in the tree, crossed the rope bridge, and finally swung down to the ground using the rope hung for that purpose.

"Excellent," she said, puffing slightly. "Give me blond hair and a couple of weeks to get my vine-swinging muscles in shape, and I'll be ready to be Jane."

"You're welcome any time," said Zee, handing her the video she'd held while Olive went aloft.

"I'll begin my training at home this afternoon by having a beer and watching this movie," said Olive, tucking the video into her purse. "I was just a kid when

I saw it on the late, late show, but I remember that it was great and made me want to go live in Africa. Speaking of kids, yours are a pair of lively ones. Nice too."

"We like them," said Zee, "so we're going to keep them."

"What's the latest in the Highsmith business?" I asked. "We've read what the papers have had to say, but that's all we know."

"I kind of expected you to show up at the station and keep your nose in the case," said Olive.

"No," I said. "I'm done with it. But I'm interested in the aftermath."

"If you're looking for a happy ending, don't hold your breath," said Olive. "Well, you know that Abigail Highsmith is out of intensive care, and that they found Henry Highsmith's bike in the quarry along with the Shelkrotts inside their car. The ME hasn't made it official yet, but I can tell you they'd both been shot by a small-caliber gun. Our guess is that it's the Colt Woodsman we found in the Willet house and that it's the same gun that killed Highsmith, but the lab people will let us know for sure."

"Any prints on the gun?"

"Officially, no comment; unofficially, there are some on the magazine."

"Whose?"

"Willet's and some others."

"The kids'?"

She shrugged. "I hope so. It would make things simpler."

"The kids still in jail?"

"Oh, no," said Olive. "Out on bail. They were only in for assaulting a police officer. That's not enough to keep anybody in jail."

It is a common complaint among police that the

perps they put in jail are often back on the street before
the cops get back to the station. It's one reason that
some cops get cynical; the real wonder is that more of
them aren't.

"Will they be charged with murder?" I asked.

"Who knows? That's up to the DA. My guess is that
they will be, because it's a high-profile case and the DA
is ambitious. It'll depend on what the lab tells us, I
think, although there may be enough circumstantial
evidence to bring charges."

"Any prints in the Mitsubishi?"

"Plenty, but they don't mean much because the kids
learned to drive in it. However," Olive raised a faux-
theatrical forefinger, "there is a development that you
haven't read about yet: they found blood residue in
the back of the Mitsubishi. You couldn't see it with the
naked eye because somebody worked hard to scrub it
away, but the lab people used fluorescein and came up
with latent bloodstains. Now they're doing a DNA com-
parison with Henry Highsmith's blood. If there's a
match, the DA is probably in business." Olive looked at
her watch. "Well, I gotta go. I'm looking forward to seeing Tarzan again. One of the nice things about this
movie, as I recall, is that justice triumphed in the end. I
like that."

She drove away.

"An ugly business," said Zee.

"We'll see how it turns out," I said.

We looked at our children climbing through the
branches of the big beech tree, testing their balance
and their grip on small limbs while we kept our tongues
from continually warning them to be careful. I wondered if the Highsmith children had ever been so innocent and then had a moment when I wondered if my
own children were as innocent as they looked.

I knew of no Mad Jacksons or of madmen or -women among Zee's Azorean ancestors, but who could say if that made any difference? Would Zee's nurture and mine define Joshua's and Diana's future, or had nature already created their destinies? Would they be tigers or lambs?

I wished, not for the first time, that I believed in a cosmos that had meaning, wherein all things were purposeful even though I might not understand that purpose.

But I didn't. What I had instead was a universe that was beautiful and vast and full of wonder, wherein I could feel awe and hope and love, if not meaning. That would have to be enough, and it usually was.

A couple of days later, Olive Otero drove into the yard and returned *Tarzan and the Leopard Woman*.

"Well," I said, "how was it?"

"Great," said Olive, "but to tell you the truth, it wasn't quite as great as I remembered it as being." She smiled. "But then, that's probably true about a lot of memories. Just as well, I imagine."

"I think you're right. Care for a beer?"

"I don't mind if I do," said Olive.

In late July, the district attorney, armed with forensic evidence, charged Gregory and Belinda Highsmith with multiple murders, including patricide.

About the same time I got a call from Glen Norton, who by then had gotten over his shakes and was back to hacking his way around Waterwoods.

"You see that damned letter in the *Times* yesterday?" Glen shouted in my ear. "Who the hell is that guy to say that stuff about Pin Oaks? People like that ought to live at the North Pole instead of America if they don't like golf courses! I'll bet the SOB is one of those blasted bike riders too!"

"I saw the letter," I said, "but I don't know if the guy rides a bike."

"Say, what I'm calling about is that Jasper and Gabe are coming over this weekend for a game. We need a fourth. You interested?"

Everything changes; nothing changes.

"Sure," I said. "Why not? Zee's been telling me that I need to get more exercise."

"I don't know how much exercise you'll get. You'll be riding a cart."

"I won't tell her that part," I said.

THREE RECIPES

J.W. and Zee cook these dishes for breakfast, but they're delish any time of day!

LOBSTER, CROISSANTS, AND CHAMPAGNE

The name says it all. J.W. and Zee have this once or twice a year and it's always a success.

One 1 1/2-lb. lobster per person
As many croissants as the breakfasters can eat
As much champagne as people want to drink

Boil the lobsters. When done, use shears to cut open the bodies, legs, and claws and serve the lobsters with croissants, champagne, and lots of melted butter, napkins, and paper towels. Lobster bibs are recommended if you're eating in anything but your bathing suit or in nothing at all.

ASPARAGUS PIE

Filling:
1 c. shredded mild cheddar cheese (preferably white)
1/2 c. good mayonnaise
1 tsp. lemon juice
1 1/2 c. asparagus (cooked to crisp-tender and cut into bite-size pieces)
Slivered almonds

Crust:
> *1 c. flour*
> *2 tsps. baking powder*
> *1/4 tsp. salt*
> *1/4 c. vegetable shortening (such as Crisco)*
> *1/2 c. cold milk*
> *Dijon mustard*

Mix dry ingredients together. Cut in shortening until mixture consists of small, crumblike particles. Stir in milk and mix lightly (do not overmix).

Roll out dough to fit a nine-inch pie pan. Spread crust with a small amount of mustard.

Mix filling ingredients together and pour into biscuit-dough crust. Bake in preheated 350-degree oven for about a half hour. The pie may be covered and frozen before baking. Thaw completely before baking.

Makes 6 servings

BRETON CREPES

Breton Crepes can be filled or garnished with a variety of foods, depending on the time of day you are serving them. Jeff and Zee enjoy them simply served with Breton Herb Butter (recipe follows).

> *1 c. plus 2 tbs. buckwheat flour*
> *1 egg*
> *1 teaspoon sea salt*
> *Water*

Put the flour in a mixing bowl, leaving a small hollow in the center. Put the egg and the salt in the hollow.

Mix with a wooden spoon, adding water little by little until the mixture is the consistency of thick mayonnaise. Mix energetically for about 10 minutes. Add more water while mixing to obtain a final consistency of cream. This may take some experimentation but is no more difficult than making regular crepes.

Ladle or pour a small amount of batter into a hot, very lightly greased skillet and quickly rotate the pan so that the batter covers the bottom evenly. When the edges start to lift away from the pan, turn carefully with a spatula and cook the other side just until lightly browned.

Crepes should not be crispy. Stir the batter frequently to keep the proper consistency.

Makes about 24 six-inch crepes

BRETON HERB BUTTER

Parsley
Chervil
Chives
Watercress
Shallot
Garlic
Pepper
Lightly salted butter

Finely chop any or all of the above and mix with lightly salted butter. The Breton Herb Butter should have a nice green color. It can be slathered on plain Breton Crepes or used to enhance other fillings.

Optional fillings or garnishes

Egg
Smoked fish or sausage
Cheese
Cooked fruits
Fruit preserves
Sardines
Soft cheese
Tomato slices with fresh herbs

ABOUT THE AUTHOR

Philip R. Craig grew up on a small cattle ranch south-east of Durango, Colorado. He earned his MFA at the University of Iowa Writers' Workshop and was for many years a professor of literature at Wheelock College in Boston. He and his wife live on Martha's Vineyard. His website is www.philiprcraig.com.